No Greater Evil

AND

No Greater Wickedness

MICHAEL ELIA

First published 2024
by Rowanvale Books Ltd
The Gate
Keppoch Street
Roath
Cardiff
CF24 3JW
www.rowanvalebooks.com

A CIP catalogue record for this book is available from the British
Library.
ISBN: 978-1-914422-83-6
eBook ISBN: 978-1-914422-82-9

NO GREATER EVIL

It was May 2020. On North Timlook's Turin Street, FBI agents Dave Bradley and James Mitchell were staking out the National Pennsylvania Bank. Agents Tony Selma, Dale Manuchi and Melissa Morgan had visited the call center and detected a phone call between arms dealers Luis Calvera and Ramon Batista discussing a hit their gang had planned against this bank.

"The call definitely mentioned this bank?" Dave asked.

"They definitely did," Jim replied.

"And phone calls don't lie."

"Except if they distort somebody's voice."

"But Tony, Dale and Melissa know Luis Calvera and Ramon Batista certainly made those calls," Dave explained. "Especially Tony, who was with me in Miami two months ago trying to nail these two arms dealers, and he would recognize their voices. Which means Calvera and Batista and a new mob of Cuban arms dealers are here in Pennsylvania. And a truck is about to crash into this bank. We've got company."

Dave and Jim reached for their handguns as the truck ploughed with devastating ferocity and crushing impact through the bank's wall, coming from the street.

"Everybody, hit the floor!" Jim yelled.

Men, women and children sprawled on the concrete floor as the bank staff dived behind their desks, and Jim opened fire. He pumped five deafening gunshots into the driver and the two other men in the front seats. They jerked backward in their seats and then fell toward the steering wheel and the windshield. They died in a matter of seconds. Five other Cubans stormed out of the back of the truck and into the bank, their beards as thick as Dave's and Jim's, their rifles more lethal than the agents' handguns. Jim pressed home his counter-attack, blasting five shots into two of these men so they fell against the other three. These three blazed eight shots toward Jim. The rounds slammed into his chest and solar plexus, and he died instantly. Dave dropped to the floor, firing with his own weapon.

Nine shots killed the attackers in two or three seconds, bloodying their chests. All five men lay splayed on the floor in pools of blood, whilst the men in the truck's front seats were slumped in an undignified manner against the steering wheel and windshield.

"Okay, it's safe to get up now!" Dave cried. "Jim! Oh Jesus Christ! Fucking Jesus! No, no, no!"

Jim's bloodied body lay on the concrete floor, his mouth agape, his big, dilated eyes staring up toward the ceiling, his expression a hideous grimace. All the customers and bank staff ascended from the floor and from bchind their desks. They gathered around Dave to help him press down on Jim's rib cage. One man searched for a first aid box; another tilted Jim's head back to open his airway.

"He won't make it," the guy said.

"No, he won't," Dave stammered. "Oh my God!" He reached inside his leather jacket for a cellphone.

***

Jim's body was taken away on a stretcher, inside a squad van, to Timlook PD's science lab for an autopsy. The eight dead Cubans were bunched up in eight body bags and their DNA collected, whilst their rifles were driven to the Forensics Lab. Dave's wife, Nicole Lamenski, now fifty-two with grey hair, approached the fifty-year-old Quaker detective. Dave still wore blond hair and a medium-length beard. Nicole was captain of Timlook PD. FBI Agent Tony Selma, walking beside her, was twenty-seven with short blond hair, a moustache and glasses; both of them were dressed in black suits. Coming behind them were homicide detectives Dale Manuchi, aged forty-seven, and Melissa Morgan, aged forty-nine, both wearing gray suits, but they still looked young with dark hair. Dale resembled the British DJ Jamie Theakston and wore a beard like Dave and Jim, whilst Melissa was the spitting image of the American actress Sheila Kelley, who starred in L.A. Law, The Jennie Project and Lost. Melissa's hair was tied back in a ponytail, exposing her forehead and shy-looking features.

Tears flowed down Melissa's face when she heard the news of Jim's death, and Nicole and Dave were also crying.

"I can't believe this has happened," Melissa said. Her teeth were clenched and her eyes sharp.

"I knew Jim for near twenty-six years, going back to the Klaus Rheitag Case in 1994," Dave told the women.

"I knew him for longer, before you started working at Timlook PD," Nicole pointed out. "Like you, Jim always had nine lives like a cat. But today, his last life ran out."

"It could've been your husband," Tony added.

"It could've been me," Dave agreed.

"We're still holding the fort at Homicide," Dale explained. "Melissa and I were wondering how you and Tony are getting on in the FBI. We miss you with a passion."

"Not as much as I miss Dave," Nicole said.

"Our marriage has lasted for twenty-five years," Dave commented.

"It's stood the test of time," Tony told them.

"Jim's body and those of the eight Cubans must be being autopsied by now," Melissa added.

"The ballistics report, the tracing of their weapons' serial numbers and their DNA profiles will link them to the arms dealers who sold them the rifles," Dale explained.

"How do you know these bank raiders were Cubans?" Nicole asked Dave.

"I told Tony on my cellphone they were Cubans, and he passed this info on to Dale and Melissa," he said.

"But Tony knew already," Melissa replied.

"From the Chief Gary Mills murder case in Miami two months ago," Tony explained. "Dave and I smashed two arms rings run by Cuban arms dealers Luis Calvera and Ramon Batista, who murdered Chief Mills's killers, two dirty cops, then escaped in a helicopter. Here in Timlook, we traced incriminating calls until we detected Calvera and Batista ordering the bank job. Then we passed on this info to Dave and Jim, and they lay in wait inside the National Pennsylvania Bank."

"One question, Dave," Nicole said.

"Go on."

"Why were only two of you staking out the bank? You should've called for backup."

"Jim and I underestimated the number of Cubans who would pull the smash-and-grab operation," Dave replied. "And too many cops, even in plain clothes, would arouse the Cubans' suspicions. But now I know this was an unforgivable mistake, and Jim paid a very high price for it. Inspector James Mitchell, being a rank above me, told me only two of us would stake out the bank to avoid blowing our cover, but I was complicit in agreeing with Jim's decision."

"You never questioned his decision?" Nicole inquired.

"No, Nicole."

"Jim was always one for being gung-ho and not expecting backup in stakeouts," Nicole told him. "You mustn't beat yourself up about what happened."

"I will beat myself up," Dave said. "Jim was my partner for so many years. I should've predicted that one day, his unorthodox methods and gung-ho mentality would catch up with him. But he was a good cop, the best of the best. He did not deserve to pay the price he paid, and we must nail his killers."

"You want to take time off first and receive counselling from a shrink?" Nicole asked.

"No, there ain't time. My first destination will be the call center where Milan Street meets Naples Street. I must assess that incriminating call Luis Calvera made to Ramon Batista."

Nicole turned to Tony, Dale and Melissa. "Do any of you want time off or counselling?"

"No, Captain Lamenski," Dale told her.

"Me neither, Captain," Melissa replied.

"Nor me," Tony said. "We owe it to Jim to bring his killers to justice."

"And we'll never rest until this is done," Melissa said. She paused.

"You bet your money Calvera and Batista were responsible," Dale butted in.

"Yes, I do, honey," Melissa said. "They sent those Cubans over to ram that truck into the bank and grab the money. But Dave and Jim were more than a match even for eight Cubans armed like marines."

"They were armed like marines," Dave agreed.

"Which means they weren't drug dealers or normal bank robbers," Tony said.

"They were arms dealers," Dave told everybody. "Their rifles were Kalashnikovs and AK-47 assault rifles, which only terrorists or arms dealers would possess. Three men with Kalashnikovs fired the fatal shots that killed Jim. That's after he shot and killed three guys in the truck's front seats, and then two guys coming from the main compartment. Before the three men behind these guys murdered Jim, and then I gunned them down."

"Bringing down five hardened criminals before you popped the other three," Dale remarked. "Jim was a real tough guy. And smart too."

"The best of the best," Melissa said. "The best cop in Timlook."

"But Dave almost matched his caliber," Tony cut in.

"He more than matched Jim's caliber," Nicole enthused.

"Thanks for the compliment," Dave chuckled.

"The four of you must support each other on this case," Nicole ordered. "First, drop in on the call center. Dig up any clues or new information on the arms dealers' call ordering the hit. Then you make your way to the forensics department, then the computer room. Read the ballistics report on those rifles before ferreting through the DNA database for info on those eight Cubans, like where they lived. The rifles' serial numbers will betray the dealers. You four must persevere."

"We're on it," Dave confirmed.

***

At the call center, the detectives studied Calvera's call to Batista. And in the background, Dave heard splashing sounds.

"There are waves beating a beach in the background," Dave said. "Which means

Calvera made the call from the East Coast, either in Pennsylvania or Maryland. I hear seagulls." He turned to Tony, Dale and Melissa. "About what time did Calvera call Batista? And did you trace Batista's reply call?"

"We did," Dale replied. "Calvera called Batista yesterday morning at ten."

"Ten a.m.," Melissa told Dave. "And that's not all."

"By the airplane noises in the background, we know Batista's reply call came from an airport," Tony pointed out.

"But not an airport for airliner planes," Dave added.

"How do you know?" Tony asked.

"Airliners with more powerful engines give out deafening noises as loud as thunder or a storm," Dave pointed out. "These noises are low, droning sounds from smaller planes, probably used to carry drugs and weapons, not passengers. And I hear wind blowing in the trees. Trees would be far away from an airport for airliners. But not an airfield in the remote countryside where drug dealers or arms dealers are using smaller planes to carry lethal drugs or deadly weapons."

"More likely weapons than drugs," Melissa remarked. "We know that during the conversation between Calvera and Batista, one was at the coast and the other in the countryside. We've narrowed down both locations even more, to within two thirty-yard radiuses. Calvera's call came from a beach a mile north of Baltimore in Maryland. Batista's reply came from five miles west of that beach—not even at an aerodrome, but a remote field where the arms dealers land their planes, probably close to their hideout. They wouldn't be stupid enough to store and load weapons at an aerodrome, which would attract the attention of law enforcement officers all over Maryland. So they used a remote field.

"You three must drop in at the science lab to collect the ballistics report and the Cubans' DNA profiles, and run these profiles through the DNA database to discover the guys' names and addresses, in Pennsylvania, Virginia or Maryland. I'll phone the Baltimore Police Department and request that they send a squad of heavily armed cops to this airfield. Something new might come up, yet I reckon our investigation will take us to Baltimore."

Dave, Tony and Dale bade farewell to Melissa and left the call center.

***

At the science lab, the pathologist and the weapons analyst approached Dave, Tony and Dale.

"These are the DNA samples from the eight Cubans Dave and Jim gunned down," the pathologist began. "Jim's body lies in the morgue."

"The rifles' serial numbers traced the weapons to two Cuban arms dealers living outside Baltimore in Maryland," the weapons analyst said, "by the names of Luis Calvera and Ramon Batista. They live in the remote countryside, on an estate called Ontario Drive three miles northwest of Baltimore. Or they did, but that estate no longer exists. Two weeks ago, law enforcement closed in on this estate, before Calvera and Batista and their gang blew up the building in a bomb explosion. Now they've disappeared off the face of the earth."

"They can't have got far," Tony said.

"They're probably at a remote hideout, somewhere in Pennsylvania or Maryland," Dale told the weapons analyst.

"We'll see if the DNA database gives us info on those Cubans me and Jim shot and killed," Dave said.

***

Inside Timlook PD's computer room, Dave, Tony and Dale were with Nicole, running DNA checks on the bank raiders.

"This is not helpful," Dave said.

"How do you mean?" Nicole asked.

"Well take a look, Captain," Tony replied.

"I'm looking," Nicole said. "We have their names."

"But only one address, Nicole," Dale told her.

"Ontario Drive, northwest of Baltimore," Tony said. "The same address Luis Calvera and Ramon Batista lived at. It was an enormous country estate on Baltimore's northwestern outskirts, big enough to house not only Calvera, Batista and eight bank raiders but a mob of over thirty arms traffickers working for Calvera. Until the mob blew up the whole estate with explosives made from canisters of liquid fertilizer."

"Because these guys knew Maryland's law enforcement teams were pulling a sting operation against Ontario Drive," Nicole realized.

"And they're hiding out somewhere remote," Dave remarked.

"The question is where, Bradley?" Dale asked him.

"Only one way we'll find out," Melissa called from the computer room's doorway. Her long dark hair now hung down to her shoulders, not in a ponytail. "We change from our suits into casual shirts and jeans for an undercover job, take one of our civilian cars, then drive down to Maryland and drop in at Baltimore PD. We inform the chief or captain of Homicide that we're pulling an undercover operation in the remote countryside northwest of Baltimore. Without infiltrating the arms trafficking ring, we carry out reconnaissance around the northern suburbs and leave no stone unturned. Finding Calvera and Batista's mob will be like trying to find a mouse in a huge barn, but we're bound to come up with something. Are you all up to the job, guys?"

The men replied that they were.

"You'd better get onto it," Nicole told Dave. "Good luck, you four. You're doing this for Jim."

***

The civilian car speeded through Pennsylvania until it crossed the state border into Maryland. The countryside of Maryland consisted of cereal fields, thick grassy pastures and deciduous forests with broad-leaved trees, their foliage varying in color from red, orange and brown to dark green and light green.

Inside the car, Dave, Tony, Dale and Melissa were all dressed in denim Levi's jeans and casual shirts, Melissa wearing a blue denim shirt.

"Are we approaching Washington DC or Baltimore?" Dale asked.

"You're asking Dave?" Tony replied.

"We're approaching Baltimore," Dave said, "but we have another thirty miles to go."

"You know your way around Maryland," Dale remarked.

"But you're a terrible driver," Melissa laughed. "You drive too fast. Stop the car and let me drive."

"I will," Dave told her. "In any case, I must stop the vehicle and make a call to Nicole at

Timlook PD and request that Homicide run an APB on the license plate of the truck the Cubans used to bash the bank's wall in that smash-and-grab operation. This will trace the original location the truck came from. And we'll take it from there."

Dave careered the car to a halt on the curb and reached for his cellphone before dialing Timlook PD's telephone number.

***

The civilian car arrived at Baltimore PD at 11 p.m. Darkness shadowed this rough-tough city, broken only by the streetlights and the headlights of many vehicles. Garbage and noise polluted the city. Dave, Tony, Dale and Melissa were exhausted from a long drive and would have to spend the night sleeping inside this police department. Leaving the car and activating the locking mechanism, they entered the department and approached reception.

"We're FBI agents from Timlook PD, Pennsylvania," Dave began. "I'm Agent Dave Bradley. These three are Agents Tony Selma, Dale Manuchi and Melissa Morgan. May I ask who runs Baltimore PD?"

"Captain Richard Darnell," the woman in reception replied. "I'll bleep his office." She pressed the bleeper for Captain Darnell's office.

The office door opened, and a stocky, moustached black man left the small room and approached the FBI agents.

"Hi there," he said. "I'm Captain Richard Darnell, and I run this joint. What can I do for you?"

"We're FBI agents sent over here by my wife Captain Nicole Lamenski at Timlook PD, Pennsylvania," Dave said. "I'm Agent Dave Bradley. The dark-haired, bearded guy is Agent Dale Manuchi. The pretty, dark-haired woman is his wife, Agent Melissa Morgan. And this young man with blond hair, a moustache and glasses is Agent Tony Selma, my partner in operations."

"Show me your ID," Darnell ordered.

The four Feds reached inside the pockets of their jeans and displayed their ID badges.

"Are you satisfied?" Dave demanded.

"I am. But Feds come dressed in suits or FBI uniforms. You're all dressed very casual, in jeans and thick shirts. And the car outside is a civilian car, not an FBI car. You mind explaining this?"

"We're doing undercover and reconnaissance work on Baltimore's outskirts north and west of the city," Dale explained.

"Trying to nail a ruthless arms trafficking gang run by two Cubans: Luis Calvera and Ramon Batista," Tony added. "They killed several people down in Florida, and Agent Bradley and myself hunted them in Miami. But when us two and a team of vice cops pulled a sting operation at 23 Palm Lane, they escaped in a helicopter."

"They're extremely dangerous," Dave said. "They sent eight Cubans to crash their truck into a bank in Timlook, and my former partner Agent James Mitchell and I popped those guys with our handguns. But Jim was killed by three of these men. We are here now to bring Jim's killers to justice."

"A cellphone conversation, the men's DNA profiles and the rifles' serial numbers linked these men to Calvera," Tony growled.

"I phoned you, asking for your people to hit an airfield where Batista answered Calvera's call from," Melissa told the captain. "Calvera made the call from a beach a mile north of Baltimore, and Batista replied to the call five miles west of the beach, from an airfield. But it couldn't have been outside an aerodrome, as the cops and Feds would immediately target an aerodrome where weapons were being loaded onto airplanes. Most likely Kalashnikovs and AK-47s, the same rifles used on that raid against the National Pennsylvania Bank in Timlook. The hit operation in which Jim was killed. Did your people pull that sting operation on the airfield, Darnell?"

"We did," Darnell said. "And it turns out all of you were wrong."

"We were wrong?!" Melissa said, shocked.

"Wrong about what?" Dale wanted to know.

"Batista answered Calvera's cell call at ten a.m. yesterday from an aerodrome overlooking an airfield," Darnell replied.

"Oh my God!" Melissa exclaimed, aghast. "Didn't this arouse your suspicions before?"

"And is Melissa right about Batista's guys loading Kalashnikovs and AK-47 assault rifles on the planes?" Dale asked.

"If so, why didn't witnesses at the aerodrome report this to the Maryland authorities?" Tony demanded.

"It did not arouse our suspicions," Darnell replied, "for we had nothing to be suspicious about. That answers Melissa's question."

"How about you answer Dale and Tony's questions," Dave said.

"In answer to Dale's question," Darnell began, "Batista's guys weren't loading Kalashnikovs, AK-47s or any other type of rifles onto the planes. Or submachine guns, handguns, revolvers, bombs or grenades. Being at an aerodrome, the planes were transport and fighter planes dating from World War Two, and the Korean and Vietnam Wars. They were too small to carry crates of guns, weapons and ammunition. Batista was alone without his gang backing him up, and he was more than a hundred meters away from the airfield where the planes took off. He had nothing to do with these planes.

"The planes may have made background noise, but Calvera and Batista are using trucks, not airplanes, to transport their men and weapons. Like that truck which rammed into the bank in Timlook.

"Which brings me to Tony's question. Why didn't witnesses at the aerodrome report this to the Maryland authorities? The simple answer is there was nothing criminal to report. There were no weapons, the planes were not suitable for carrying guns and ammo, and Batista went nowhere near these planes. People at the aerodrome probably had no knowledge Batista was a criminal, because he just came across as a normal spectator."

"All this makes sense," Dave said. "Calvera and Batista are using trucks to carry men and rifles. They would have no need to use planes. That truck carrying those eight Cubans who attacked the National Pennsylvania Bank drove all the way to Timlook from eastern Pennsylvania or Maryland. It's a good thing I stopped our car on the way to Baltimore to call Nicole and ask Timlook Homicide to do an APB on that truck's number plate."

"Why an APB?" Darnell asked.

"To trace where in Pennsylvania, Virginia or Maryland the truck came from," Dave replied, "we narrow down the original location of the truck, and this will lead us to Calvera and Batista and their gang. But I'm waiting for Nicole to get back to me."

"One question," Darnell said. "The mob numbers over thirty guys against just the four of you. How do you plan to bring them down?"

"We don't," Dave remarked. "When we close in on Calvera's guys, we'll call your guys over from Baltimore PD and Maryland's branch of the FBI. Tomorrow morning, we'll skip breakfast, and Dale and Melissa will visit the aerodrome to question witnesses who may have seen Batista answering Calvera's call on his mobile. Agent Selma and I will begin reconnaissance work in the countryside north and west of Baltimore. See if anything new turns up that leads us to Calvera and Batista. Then I'll arrange a meeting point to rendezvous with Agents Manuchi and Morgan.

"Tonight, we'll buy takeout and drinks, and then spend the night here at Baltimore PD, catching up on some sleep."

"Be careful, guys," Darnell said. "And you, Agent Manuchi."

"We will," Melissa replied.

"You can count on that," Dave told him.

"Get some food," Darnell ordered.

***

The FBI agents slept from midnight until 7 a.m. Early in the morning, Dave was awoken by his cell bleeping. The loud noise also woke up Tony, Dale and Melissa. Dave answered the phone, raising it to his face and touching his beard.

"Hello there. Who is it?"

"Is that you, Dave?" Nicole asked. "It's Captain Nicole Lamenski calling from Timlook PD. How's your investigation going?"

"We haven't even started," Dave answered. "Did your people do an APB on that truck's license plate?"

"Do you have a pen and paper?" Nicole wanted to know.

"I'll get them—they're on the desk." Dave rose to his feet and grabbed the pen and paper. "I'm ready, Nicole."

"The APB traced the truck to a junkyard three miles north of Baltimore PD. It's called 'The Chandler and Co. Business' and it specializes in large trucks. You got that, honey?"

"I got it. I have to go now. Goodbye, Nicole."

Nicole cut off contact.

"The Chandler and Co. Business." Dave finished off writing down the name. "Three miles north of Baltimore PD."

Tony, Dale and Melissa were awake.

"Chandler and Co.!" Dale exclaimed, seeing what Dave had written.

"What's that?" Melissa asked.

"It's three miles north of Baltimore PD," Tony replied.

"It's a business dealing in heavy vehicles like trucks," Dave explained. "The APB on the Cubans' truck traced the vehicle's origins to this business's junkyard. Tony and I will interrogate the owners."

Captain Darnell entered the main office, having overheard their conversation.

"You drove to Baltimore in only one civilian car," Darnell told the FBI agents. "You and Tony can use that car to drop in on the junkyard. Dale and Melissa will take one of our civilian cars to drive to the aerodrome."

"Thanks, Captain," Dave said.

***

Driving in one of Baltimore PD's vehicles, Dale and Melissa pulled up in the aerodrome's car park. They vacated the car and locked it with an electronic key. They approached the manager inside the bar area.

"Hi there," the manager greeted them. "Have you come to watch our planes pulling stunts in the air? Planes dating from the Second World War, and the wars in Korea and Vietnam?"

"No, we're on police business," Melissa explained. "We're FBI agents, and these are our badges to prove it. I'm Agent Melissa Morgan."

"Agent Dale Manuchi," Dale told the manager. "Melissa is my wife. We're dressed casual because we're carrying out undercover and reconnaissance work to find two arms dealers called Luis Calvera and Ramon Batista. They were behind a bank raid in Timlook, Pennsylvania, but the eight Cubans working for Calvera were foiled by two FBI agents. One of the agents died. The day before, at ten a.m., Batista was here receiving a cellphone call from Calvera. Calvera ordered Batista to send these Cubans to Timlook.

"At first, we thought Batista and his mob were loading rifles onto planes, not knowing this was an aerodrome with planes that are not suitable for carrying crates of rifles and ammo. We thought these planes took the Cubans and their rifles to some trucks somewhere in eastern or southeastern Pennsylvania before one of these trucks was used in the bank raid. But now we know the arms trafficking gang only use trucks to carry mobsters and weapons. And an APB on the truck's license plate traced the vehicle to a junkyard business in Baltimore. A junkyard that sells trucks. Witnesses claim they saw nothing suspicious, except a guy receiving a cellphone call from a few miles away. Did you see this guy?"

"Yes, I did," the manager said.

"What did he look like?"

"Of medium height, stocky with long black hair and a beard. By his accent, I could tell he was Cuban, not Mexican or Puerto Rican. The guy looked stern and serious, and there was tension in his voice."

"That was Ramon Batista." Dale nodded. "Talking to Calvera."

"Did you notice anything else?" Melissa wanted to know. "Like eight bearded Cubans with Kalashnikovs and AK-47s standing near a truck—the rifles used in that bank raid? The mob won't know you spoke to us, so don't be scared."

"I did," the manager told them. "There were eight men like you described outside a truck in the car park. After the phone call, Batista ordered these guys to hit a bank in Timlook. But even if those guys died in that attack, the man you call Batista, his fellow arms dealer Calvera and their mob are still at large. So this interview never happened. Can you promise me that?"

The FBI agents agreed to keep everything confidential.

***

At The Chandler and Co. Business, Dave and Tony drove Timlook PD's civilian car to the curb outside the entrance, where a sign displayed the business's name. The FBI agents vacated the car, locked the vehicle and then ambled through the archway with the sign above. The junkyard was teeming with secondhand trucks sold to Chandler and Co. by delivery businesses and military camps who no longer wanted these vehicles.

But the trucks were in brilliant condition, still fit to be used by organized criminals to carry armed men, drugs and weapons.

"Let me do all the talking," Dave suggested.

"I will," Tony said.

"I don't trust these men," Dave told him.

They approached a gang of six rough-looking men with brutal faces, who walked menacingly toward them.

"I have a really bad feeling about this," Tony said.

"So do I."

"Should we go for our handguns?"

"No, Tony. Just play it cool."

The six men surrounded the detectives.

"You are trespassing!" the manager snarled.

"Are you the manager, Chandler?" Dave growled. "We're FBI agents. I'm Agent Dave Bradley. This is Agent Tony Selma. We're investigating a truck used in a bank raid in Timlook, and the APB on the truck traced its original location to The Chandler and Co. Business. No doubt you sold this truck to Cuban arms traffickers who used it in the bank raid. You are Chandler, are you not?"

"The name's Robert Chandler. And you ain't got no business meddling in our operations."

"Meddling in your operations? Meaning criminal operations linked to an arms trafficking gang under Luis Calvera and Ramon Batista? We'll leave you alone if you tell us which address in Maryland you sold the truck to. If you refuse, we'll break into your office and go through your records to find the address. But you can make it easy for all of us by showing us the address in the register with records of addresses."

"You have a hell of a nerve, you motherfucker!" Chandler shouted. He seized Dave by the collar, but Dave grabbed his thumbs and violently twisted his hands around and downward, the sudden force breaking his wrists, before wrenching the man's fingers back, breaking them. Chandler screamed with hellish agony before Dave kneed him in the groin and sent him sprawling on the ground.

The other five guys closed in, but Dave and Tony sprang into action before the men could beat them up. Two guys threw their fists toward Dave and Tony, but both FBI agents caught the men's arms, twisted them violently and dislocated their shoulders.

The men screamed hysterically, bone-breaking agony bellowing in their roaring voices. A third man came at Dave. With his kung fu, Dave smashed a sideways kick into the pressure point above the guy's knee, breaking his right leg. Roaring with agony, the brute dropped to the floor. The last two men attacked Tony, but Tony's karate training was just as formidable as Dave's kung fu. A savage punch to the throat snapped a man's windpipe. He gasped, clutching his throat, and fell to the ground, dying in the next ten seconds. Before the man died, Tony threw his fist into the other man's face, splitting open his jaw, shearing all his bottom teeth off at the gum and sending a spray of blood billowing into the air. Tony's next punch rammed into the guy's solar plexus, rupturing his guts, upsetting the nerves and striking the lower region of the heart. His diaphragm was punctured and his nerves died as shock ran through his heart and pancreas. The man collapsed and died two or three seconds later.

Dave and Tony yanked out their handguns and fired several shots into the three men still alive: two with dislocated shoulders, the third with a broken leg. These guys died instantly.

Only Robert Chandler remained, writhing in appalling agony from his two broken wrists, all his fingers broken and the knee to his groin. He screamed with terror.

"No, no, don't kill me!" Chandler yelled.

"Then tell us the address you sold the truck with these numbers on!" Dave cried. "The numbers on the license plate!"

"The Timber Wolf Roadhouse!"

"Where in Baltimore is that?" Dave demanded.

"Five miles northwest of Baltimore!" Chandler cried. "In the countryside!"

"I'll write that down," Tony said. With a pen and paper, he recorded the address.

But despite having two fractured wrists and ten broken fingers, Chandler seized a handgun from his jacket pocket and aimed toward Dave and Tony. Taking the initiative, Dave squeezed the trigger of his own handgun and blazed three fierce bursts.

The gunshots punched into Chandler's chest and solar plexus, killing him in seconds. Blood gushed from his wounds as he lay splayed in an undignified manner, his mouth agape, his eyes wide with death.

"He may have lied about the address just to put us off the trail," Tony told Dave.

"One way we'll find out," Dave said.

"How is that?"

"We check the register in the office."

***

Tony was inside the civilian car, waiting for Dave. Then Dave opened the driver's door, dropped into the seat and closed the door before turning to Tony.

"He was telling the truth."

"The Timber Wolf Roadhouse," Tony said. "Five miles north of Baltimore."

"Five miles northwest of Baltimore. I'll call Dale and Melissa now." Dave reached for his mobile and dialed Dale's number.

"Hi there, Dale Manuchi here."

"Who's calling?" Melissa asked in the background. "Is that Dave?"

"It's me," Dave responded. "Meet us at the Timber Wolf Roadhouse, five miles northwest of Baltimore."

"Five miles northwest of Baltimore?" Dale inquired. "At which landmark?"

"I'll find a map on my cellphone," Tony called. He showed Dave a map with a copse of aspen trees behind the roadhouse. "It is in front of a copse of aspen trees named Rickshaw Woods."

"Rickshaw Woods?" Melissa asked. "Five miles northwest of Baltimore?"

"We got that," Dale told them. "I have to charge up my cellphone. We're on our way."

Dale hung up.

"Let's go," Dave growled.

***

Dave's civilian car arrived on a side road two hundred yards from the Timber Wolf Roadhouse twenty minutes before Dale's vehicle. Dave and Tony waited.

"There's a number of trucks outside that roadhouse," Dave whispered.

"I hope Dale and Melissa find us," Tony said.

"They will."

"How do you know?" Tony snapped.

"I just know. And when they climb into the car's back seats, we'll abandon Baltimore PD's civilian car and only take this car. We're all safer grouped together in one vehicle than separated into two vehicles. And what's happening now? They're coming toward our vehicle and are about to open the back doors."

Both doors opened and Dale and Melissa hurried into the back seats before shutting the doors with force.

"Hi guys," Melissa enthused. "We found you at last."

"Shall we make our move?" Dale asked.

"We will," Dave said.

"And let's have our handguns ready," Tony suggested.

All four FBI agents entered the Timber Wolf Roadhouse, each holding their handgun in both hands. The bar area was full of drunken Cubans and Americans who were casually dressed and rough-looking with beards or moustaches. They were laughing in a sinister manner.

"Excuse us," Dale shouted.

"You enjoying yourselves, guys?" Melissa chuckled. "It's quite a carnival here."

"Don't draw attention to yourself, honey," Dale replied.

"It's business, not pleasure," Tony told them.

"What kind of business?" a bearded man shouted.

"We're looking for Luis Calvera and Ramon Batista," Dave yelled. "You know where they are?"

"Out of town! What kind of business?"

"This kind!" Melissa yelled, pointing her handgun in his face.

Dale, Tony and Dave aimed their handguns at the other brutes.

"Don't try anything stupid!" Dale shouted.

"Or you're dead!" Melissa cried.

"I have a question," Dave said. "Where are Calvera and Batista?"

But Melissa's opponent grabbed her wrists and deflected her weapon away from his face. And he had the misfortune to be up against a woman who had spent a few years practicing karate before joining Timlook Homicide, then many years training and using martial arts and self-defense on the street. Melissa used her weight and leverage behind her wiry arms to turn the guy's arms downward so his upper body and head bent toward the floor, then pulled the trigger so a gunshot penetrated his leg. The man screamed in excruciating pain before she kneed him twice in the stomach then swung a violent kick into his hips. The guy fell, and Melissa shot him in the back of the head. The other mobsters threw chairs at her and her male colleagues, but Dave, Dale and Tony started firing. Five blasts from Dave's piece felled three Americans just as four from Tony's weapon brought down two Cubans, and Dale fired six times into three Cubans, flooring them in pools of blood. Melissa was also blazing with fury, pumping five exploding shots into two other Americans. Their chests plastered with blood, they all fell to the floor.

The mass of Americans and Cubans fled for their lives, diving through open windows, out of the front and back doorways or into the washroom. But a vast mass of twenty bearded or moustached Cubans had no fear, as their truck crashed through the roadhouse's front wall and windows. Dave and Tony saw Calvera and Batista sitting in the front seats, Calvera driving the huge vehicle. The massive gang of rough-tough men with high-caliber rifles stormed out of the truck's compartment and into the demolished building.

"There's too many of them!" Tony yelled.

"Run!" Dave cried. "The window over there!"

The FBI agents sprinted toward the enormous window, leaped up onto the windowsill and hurtled outside onto a side path.

Four rough-looking bearded Americans were at the end of the path, focusing their rifles. Dave blasted toward two men with the same rage and fury that Dale and Tony blazed at two others. All four criminals fell in bloodied heaps. Dave, Tony, Dale and Melissa continued running down the side road toward Timlook PD's civilian car. Dave deactivated the locking mechanism; they wrenched the doors open and scrambled inside. Two trucks closed in on the car from the destroyed roadhouse, each vehicle's front seats accommodating two men. Tony and Dale aimed their handguns toward the truck to the right and Dave and Melissa took the truck to the left. Several gunshots from Tony and Dale killed the two men in the right truck, and Dave and Melissa felled the two guys in the left truck, Dave taking out the driver and Melissa the guy beside him.

All four men slumped onto the windshields before the trucks ground to a halt, their tires screeching on the tarmac.

"We got these scum!" Melissa shouted.

"But we're still in danger!" Dale cried.

"Other men are running toward the trucks!" Dave said.

"Get out of here!" Tony yelled.

"You bet we will!"

Racing the car around in a U-turn, Dave accelerated toward the end of the side road, then sped along the highway leading east and then north.

"The mob are too many for us to take on!" Tony screamed.

"Our time will come!" Dave shouted. "They're right behind us and will pursue us through Maryland and into Pennsylvania."

"You told Captain Darnell we would get his guys to back us up!" Dale yelled.

"That's not an option now!"

"They're too far away in Baltimore!" Dale agreed.

"You got it, honey!" Melissa cried.

"In any case!" Dave began. "Calvera's mob will make mincemeat of Darnell's guys. Calvera has close to forty or fifty men in his syndicate, armed with high-caliber rifles like shotguns!"

Dave paused for a moment, then said, "They're on our tails! Two trucks behind us. With two drivers to replace the four guys we shot and killed a few minutes ago!"

"Only one thing for it," Melissa suggested.

"Let's shoot their tires," Dale said.

Opening the back windows, he and Melissa aimed their handguns toward the trucks' tires, Dale focusing on the right truck's right front wheel whilst Melissa pointed her weapon at the left truck's left front wheel. Their first two or three gunshots missed, but the next three slugs from Dale's piece ruptured the right wheel's tire, sending jets of air billowing out and causing the truck to veer off at an angle. Two more rounds from Melissa's gun punctured the other truck's left tire, and the truck careered off the country road and crashed into some trees.

"We should make a clean getaway," Melissa said.

"You bet we will," Tony said.

"But these guys are now bent on murder," Dale warned Tony. "Our murders."

"Wiping out Calvera's mob is a job for the US Army," Dave told them. "The arms trafficking ring are armed like an army, and it will take an army to defeat an army."

"Especially a mob of fifty men," Tony added.

"Are you serious?" Dale asked. "Calling in the army!"

"They are serious, my love," Melissa told him.

"But Calvera and Batista's guys are hot on our tail," Tony said. "How do we hide from them?"

"I'll find a hiding place," Dave reassured him. "That saloon ahead of us to the left. We'll have a big lunch and do some careful planning."

"Some careful planning?" Dale repeated.

"You bet."

"You know what I suggest?" Melissa added.

"Carry on," Dale invited her.

"We don't leave Maryland," she explained. "We drive back to Baltimore or Washington D.C. and inform the army. Even if we have to walk into the White House and tell the President, only the army is strong enough to overpower a mob of forty or fifty tough guys armed with high-velocity rifles. The four of us only have handguns and only so many magazines of ammo, no electric stun guns, pepper sprays or even handcuffs."

"We don't have to go to Washington D.C.," Tony said.

"We just make our way to Baltimore," Dave added.

"You're serious about involving the army?" Dale asked, his voice sarcastic.

"We are," Tony said.

"Will they listen to us?"

"They will, honey," Melissa promised him. "It's our best bet."

"Melissa!" Dale exclaimed. "Are you a dumb bitch? You're beautiful, but you left your brain in Timlook!"

"Hey, you horrible husband!" Melissa snapped, her voice spiteful. "Don't call me a dumb bitch! I may be forty-nine going on fifty, but my brain is in good working order! As young and feminine as my beautiful face!"

"You could've fooled me!"

"Dave and Tony came up with the idea first!"

"That's right, pass the buck, young lady!" Tony snarled.

"Okay, whose idea was it?" Melissa asked. "Do you and Dale have any better ideas?"

"No, we don't!" Dale growled.

"Enough arguing, guys, ladies!" Dave cried. "It was my idea. And Tony went along with it!"

"Sorry I called you a dumb bitch," Dale told his wife.

"It's you who needs a brain transplant," Melissa snapped back.

"Oh, very funny."

"I'm serious."

"I said enough arguing!" Dave shouted. "We're at the saloon now; let's all cool down and get some lunch. It was my idea to involve the army! Once we've had an enormous meal, we'll drive back to Baltimore and twist Captain Darnell's arm. With gentle persuasion and a little bit of firmness, we'll sweet-talk Darnell to brief the army at Guanaco and Annapolis and even the CIA at Langley, Virginia. They will contact him and decide whether to pull a covert operation against Calvera and Batista's guys."

"Just like the army are used to taking out drug cartels in Colombia and Mexico," Tony suggested.

"Drug cartels, yeah," Dale agreed. "But arms traffickers? That's a job for our SWAT teams, backed up by the FBI."

"It's worth our best shot, my love," Melissa said.

"Okay, but what if the army refuses? What if even Captain Richard Darnell can't persuade them?"

"We call in the SWAT teams together with the FBI and maybe the DEA," Tony said.

"The SWAT teams are armed and heavily armored like paras or marines," Dave pointed out. "And us four will be right behind them. Now can we all stop arguing and get some lunch?"

"Yes sir," Melissa chuckled, raising her hand to her head in an army salute. "At your service, General."

"Knock it off," Dale demanded.

***

All four of them were eating large meals with their plates overflowing with food. But Melissa chomped down her food and drank her lemonade much faster than the other three and finished first. She turned to her male colleagues.

"It only took me three to five minutes to devour my meal," she told them. "I'm taking a walk in the woods for ten minutes. I'll be back, guys."

"Okay, have a great walk," Dale said.

"Don't be too long," Tony ordered.

"Make sure it's only ten minutes," Dave told her. "We'll be leaving soon."

***

Melissa came to a pond and kneeled down. She splashed water over her long hair, then swiped it back from her forehead.

It was a hot day in May and she needed to cool down by wetting her hair, forehead and face. Then she cupped her hands and poured a little water underneath her thick denim shirt, soaking her breasts and narrow shoulders. Jerking her head backward, throwing her dark hair away from her bare forehead and behind her shoulders, she was about to tie her hair back in a ponytail. But suddenly, she heard armed men shouting in Spanish. They had Cuban accents.

"Oh my God," Melissa said. "Calvera's guys are here."

She ran from the pool and through the woods.

Five minutes later, she reached the edge of the woods, and with a chill in her stomach, she watched armed Cubans pointing their rifles at Dave, Tony and Dale. The three men had their arms tied behind their backs with strong white straps. Three Cubans produced, from their leather jackets, white gags to thrust into the agents' mouths and tie behind their heads. Melissa's eyes were sharp with fear.

Two bearded Cubans sneaked up behind her; one of them grabbed her slim arms. Melissa threw a backward punch into his groin before elbowing him savagely in the stomach. She threw three violent punches into the other guy's face, bloodying his nose and mouth.

She reached inside her jeans for her handgun, but the second Cuban knocked the weapon out of her hands. With two front kicks to the man's hips, she hurled him to the grass then started running. She had to get away from this gang as quickly as possible, hide in the woods and make a mobile call to Captain Darnell at Baltimore PD.

Melissa sprinted like a greyhound, with a whole gang of armed Cubans pursuing her. Three men blazed three shots from their rifles, the bullets penetrating the aspen and maple trees around her. Melissa ran toward the pond but realized her only escape route was cut off. She doubled back and tried to circle the pond but tripped on a rock and fell over. She crawled along, and then a guy was on top of her. He pinned her arms behind her back before tying her wrists.

Melissa gritted her teeth against the pain as she felt the white strap dig into her wrists.

"Don't struggle, and you won't get hurt," the Cuban said.

"Where are you taking me?" Melissa cried. "And where are you taking my friends?"

"To two different locations," the bearded brute replied. "We're taking you just over the state border into Pennsylvania. Where Calvera's guys deal not only in guns and weapons but also drugs. Like cannabis, heroin and cocaine. We'll give you a taste. And then you'll know what pain really is."

Two moustached Cubans came up behind him. They aimed their rifles down toward Melissa.

"Don't kill her," the first guy told the other two. "She's coming with us." He pulled Melissa off the ground before his backup took both her arms and manhandled her through the woods. "Your three male friends are staying here in Maryland."

***

In a makeshift prison cell, Dave, Tony and Dale were bound and gagged, their arms strapped behind their backs around a pillar rising from the center of the floor to the ceiling. Outside the cell was an interrogation room. Dave reached his hands around and undid the buttons in the two straps tying Tony and Dale's wrists. Then he loosened both straps so they could rip off the straps and release their hands. Dale repeated this action with Dave's strap, tearing out the buttons and then pulling it loose. When the three agents were being interrogated, they would wrench their hands free, and then they would fight and subdue—or even kill—the men who were torturing them.

At that moment, a key was turned inside the door's lock and the enormous mass of wood was pushed open. Six huge men, four of them bearded and two moustached, entered the cell. They untied the gags from behind the FBI agents' heads and pulled them away from their mouths. Then they pulled the agents upwards and surrounded them. Three men held the agents in grappling holds from behind whilst the other three stood in front to rain blows and kicks into the agents' stomachs and faces.

"Do you have any water?" Dale said.

"What is that, senor?" the ringleader shouted.

"You have water?" Dale cried.

"People drink it!" Dave yelled.

"To quench their thirst!" Dale added.

"And we're thirsty!" Tony cried.

"Can we have some water?" Dave asked. "And then we'll talk!"

"You have a nerve, you Americans," the ringleader said.

"We have a nerve?" Tony objected.

"Just watch us in action!" Dave said, then swung his head backward with two head-butts to his grappler's face, fracturing his jaw and smashing all his bottom teeth in.

His mouth full of blood and broken teeth, the man hurtled toward the floor, clutching his jaw. Tony threw a backward punch into a second man's crotch just as Dale hurled two savage elbow strikes into the third guy's stomach and solar plexus. Both men writhed in excruciating agony on the floor beside the man with the broken jaw. The guy facing Dave hurled his huge fist toward Dave's face, but Dave swerved and seized the guy's arm before twisting and turning it violently, ripping the brute's shoulder out of its socket. His arm dislocated, the criminal screamed like a terrified woman before Dave smashed five punches into his face, breaking his jaw so a spurt of blood gushed from his mouth. He landed a savage kick into the thug's groin, hard enough to cripple him, before bashing both his hands into the brute's ears and then head-butting him in the face. Blood sprayed from his nose, mouth and ears. One last punch forced the bridge of his nose up into his brain, killing him instantly. The criminal dropped to the floor.

Dave's kung fu was lethal, but Tony and Dale had learned karate and self-defense techniques that were just as deadly. They seized the two guys left standing, wrenched them around and hurled them over their shoulders. Tony's opponent landed on a table and then fell to the floor just as Dale's crashed against a chair, smashing it to pieces. Pressing home their attack, they repeatedly kicked the brutes' groins and stomachs, paralyzing both mobsters and rupturing their stomachs before Dale's kicks broke one man's ribs. Dropping down, Tony and Dale pounded the Cubans' faces with their fists, but these guys were immune to pain. Despite both Cubans being crippled, their stomachs punctured and one guy's ribs being broken, they rained punches toward Tony and Dale's faces. But three blows from Dale's fist broke through ribs, puncturing the mobster's heart and killing him. Tony slammed a fast punch into the other guy's throat, breaking his windpipe. With an agonized gasp, the man died instantly.

But the three Cubans who had restrained the FBI agents had recovered, and they scrambled off the floor. Having taken a handgun from the ringleader, whom he had killed, Dave raised the weapon and blazed two deafening gunshots toward the heads of two mobsters. The bullets ripped the guys' skulls in half, blood billowing from their brains before they fell on top of Tony and

Dale. The third mobster grabbed Dale, but Dale slammed his fist into the brute's groin three times, forcing his balls into his stomach. The guy screamed hysterically and collapsed before two powerful elbow-strikes from Dale's muscular arm snapped his neck like a plank of wood. His broken neck making a horrific cracking sound that struck terror into Tony and Dale, the hardened criminal flopped to the floor like a sack of rice.

"You okay, guys?" Dave asked.

"We're okay," Dale said. "I'm fit for a man of forty-seven, and I feel as young as I look. You don't look a day over fifty."

"Like you, I don't feel it either."

"I'm a young guy in his element, backing you up," Tony told Dave. "Our martial arts skills not only enable us to kick these mobsters' butts but they also prolong our youthful appearances."

"But our nightmare is not over yet," Dale said. "We must find Melissa."

"The mobsters took our handguns," Dave said. "But I have the ringleader's gun. In the interrogation room are some rifles— high-caliber rifles. We'll take three rifles and fifteen magazines full of bullets, five magazines for each rifle. We'll load three magazines of ammo into these rifles in case we run into trouble. Then we'll steal one of their trucks, and drive back to the saloon where we had lunch."

"Drive back to the saloon?!" Tony exclaimed.

"Where's the sense in that?" Dale asked.

"We must pick up Timlook PD's civilian car," Dave explained.

"That makes sense," Dale agreed.

"We abandon the truck, drive through Maryland and find Melissa," Dave told them.

***

Opening the outside door, they sneaked out of the interrogation building, and sprinted across the yard, covering the distance in twelve seconds. They reached the gate leading outside the hideout and saw ten Cubans lying asleep. Blazing his rifle, Dave ruptured three heads while Tony punctured the heads of two guys, and two others had their heads torn open by Dale's two gunshots. The last three guys awoke and seized their own rifles, but the FBI agents struck first. A blow from Dave's rifle butt broke a criminal's windpipe so he died in seconds. Tony and Dale bashed their rifle butts into the heads of two other mobsters, splitting open their skulls and killing the brutes instantly. But four other Cubans sprinted out of the main building. This hideout had housed twenty mobsters, including the six interrogators and ten guards.

Now only four remained, and their rifles vomited a barrage of gunshots toward the FBI agents. Dave, Tony and Dale dropped onto their fronts on the ground, Dave and Dale scratching their beards, Tony rubbing his blond hair and moustache and rearranging his glasses. The Cubans' rifle shots flew over the agents' heads before they lowered their weapons to fire down at the three men. Dale blasted five gunshots into two Cubans, throwing them backward to the concrete where they perished. Tony blazed four bursts of gunfire into the third killer, bloodying his chest and solar plexus, and the man also hurtled to the ground and died. Dave repeated this volley of fire against the fourth brute, five bullets slamming into the mobster's chest and head. With blood billowing from his fatal injuries, the criminal lay splayed beside the others, his arms and legs spread out.

"What do we do now?" Dale asked.

"We get out of here," Tony said.

"Go for that truck," Dave ordered. "The one parked in the driveway behind us."

***

Just over the state border in southeastern Pennsylvania, two miles north of Maryland, was Luis Calvera's third hideout. The hideout in Ontario Drive had been destroyed by an explosion, and the Timber Wolf Roadhouse demolished by Calvera and Batista crashing a truck into the roadhouse's wall when they'd tried to corner Dave's team, but the FBI agents had escaped.

In a locked room, Melissa sat with her legs curled on a bed, her arms tied behind her back with a strong strap and her mouth gagged with white tape. It was a warm and well-lit room, the bright light shining upon her naked forehead and feminine face. Her cries muffled through the tape, she fought desperately to free herself from the strap fastened around her wrists. But the more she struggled, the more the strap dug like wire into her skin and her slim arms ached. She shook out her long dark hair and struggled again. But her efforts were futile.

Her cellphone was still in the right pocket of her jeans. Digging into her pocket, Melissa pulled out her phone, turned her head around behind her back and dialed Captain Nicole Lamenski's number. Nicole answered the call.

"Hi there, is that you, Melissa?" Nicole asked. "I know it's your cell calling me. Are you okay?"

Melissa mumbled the words, "Help, help me," through the strip of tape covering her mouth.

"Oh my God!" Nicole exclaimed. "You're in trouble! I'll trace your GPS signal and call Dave's men to come and rescue you. If you've been kidnapped, turn off your cell and put it back in your pocket before your kidnappers figure out you've called me. Hang in there."

Nicole hung up, and Melissa switched off the power button and thrust the cellphone back deep inside her pocket. Then a key was turned inside the door's lock, and the door opened. Five rough-looking guys entered the room. Melissa looked with petrified terror toward the men.

"You FBI Agent Melissa Morgan?" one of them asked.

Melissa nodded, whimpering through the tape.

"You're coming with us," another man said. They approached her, took her arms and manhandled her out of the room.

Outside in the courtyard, the Cubans pushed Melissa toward Luis Calvera and Ramon Batista.

"It's a pleasure to meet a young woman as pretty as you," Calvera laughed. "Even women down in our native Cuba don't match your insane beauty."

Still bound and gagged, Melissa refused to utter a sound, staying calm. Then Calvera's viselike hand grabbed her hair and wrenched her head back violently, so she groaned a muffled cry of agony through the tape.

"You're supposed to thank me!" Calvera screamed. "Make three sounds to show you appreciate my compliment!"

Melissa mumbled three sounds.

"We'll take her to the truck," Batista told him.

Once inside the truck, Melissa sat on the floor beside the five men. Batista was in the front seat driving. Calvera was in the back with his men, and he tore the white tape away from Melissa's mouth. She clenched her teeth with pain, the strap around her wrists still holding her arms fast behind her back.

"You can breathe," Calvera said.

"Where are you taking me?" Melissa asked.

"To the clinic in the small town of Lincoln in southern Pennsylvania," Calvera said. "But first, we'll put you in another truck, in the front seat, where we'll knock you out."

"Are you going to kill me?" Melissa whimpered. Tears flowed down her face.

"With an overdose of cocaine," Calvera told her. "But first, I'll play Russian roulette with you."

He produced his handgun and stood up before walking down the moving truck's compartment and then aiming the weapon at Melissa's head. Trying to hide her fear, Melissa clenched her teeth again and stared down the bushy-moustached brute, her eyes large with apprehension. Then she closed her mouth, her lips tight together. Calvera squeezed the trigger, but there was no gunshot. He pulled the trigger again, and the gun made another clicking sound. He repeated this three more times with the same result. Then he replaced the handgun back inside the pocket of his leather jacket.

Melissa gulped, and breathed slowly, more nervous than ever. Calvera approached her again and sank into a sitting position.

"The gun is empty," he remarked. "Not one round inside. Today is your lucky day. But your luck will run out at the Lincoln Clinic when we tell the doctors and nurses you're a psychopath who murdered one of my men. None of them will have sympathy for you, let alone help you. Two doctors under my payroll will inject an overdose of cocaine into your arm, and you'll die a slow and agonizing death. These doctors are Matt Detroit and Rudy Kosinski."

"You are sick," Melissa whined.

"Dealing in arms and drugs is a sick business," he replied.

On the country road three miles from Lincoln, the truck stopped in front of another truck on the curb. Calvera, Batista and the five armed men climbed out with Melissa, her arms still tied behind her back. Opening the second truck's front doors, Batista and the men jumped up into the main compartment, whilst Calvera lifted Melissa up into the front seat beside the driver's seat. He shut the heavy door, then ran around to the driver's side, leaped into the driver's seat and took Melissa's narrow shoulders in his huge hands.

"You won't get away with this," Melissa said.

"Sure I won't, lady," Calvera hissed.

Melissa cried out in extreme pain as he grabbed her long hair, pulled her head back and then, with savage force, bashed her forehead into the dashboard. The terrible impact jarred her brain and knocked her unconscious. She slumped toward Calvera, falling to lie across both front seats with her head on his lap.

"Okay, Lincoln," he growled. "Here we come."

***

In the civilian car, Dave, Tony and Dale were driving toward Montana Drive in Pennsylvania.

"Nicole called me," Dave said. "She received a distress signal from Melissa at Montana Drive. Nicole could tell from Melissa's mumbled voice she was bound and gagged, meaning she has been kidnapped. Nicole used Timlook PD's computers to run a GPS trace on Melissa's cellphone, and traced her call to Montana Drive, Calvera's third hideout. Then Nicole phoned me and briefed me on Melissa's whereabouts."

"Melissa has got herself out of some tight situations," Dale said. "But will she get herself out of this, in case we don't get to her in time?"

"We have yet to see," Tony said.

They stopped the car a hundred yards from Montana Drive and sprinted into the courtyard.

"There are no trucks here," Dave observed. "We'll still search."

Sneaking up toward the front door, their rifles clenched in their sweaty hands, they waited with anticipation.

"We're ready when you are," Dale told Dave.

With their combined weight and strength, they smashed the door open. But Dave realized the door was booby-trapped. A lit torch was knocked over by the door being bashed in, igniting gasoline on the carpet.

"Get out!" Dave cried.

The whole hallway and the rooms around burst into flames, for gasoline soaked the whole floor.

"I smell canisters of liquid fertilizer," Tony said.

"Which were used to blow up Ontario Drive," Dale pointed out.

"Get out of the courtyard now!" Dave yelled. "This whole place is about to blow!"

They sprinted back to the gate and then darted toward their car. Seconds later, a savage blast exploded through the whole of Montana Drive, sending wood and glass flying in all directions. Dave, Tony and Dale hid behind their vehicle just in time, avoiding the shards of glass raining down on them.

"Are you okay?" Tony asked.

"I'm okay," Dale said. "Are you, Dave?"

"I'm okay."

"That was close," Tony told them.

"Do you think Melissa was in that building?" Dale asked.

"No, Dale," Dave promised him. "The mobsters' trucks are not here. They took Melissa somewhere else. They knew Melissa had made a call to Nicole's cellphone, probably overhearing her in the next room or the hallway, even though her gag muffled her cries for help. They took her outside, left some men to rig the building to explode using a fire torch, gasoline and canisters of fertilizer, in order to massacre all three of us, then drove her to another destination. The tire tracks on the highway are so large; they were made by a truck. They're leading north. Probably toward Lincoln. We must drive in that direction."

They made their way along the highway, driving along the tire tracks, until they saw the tracks leading onto the curb.

"Stop the car," Dave ordered.

"Why, Dave?" Tony asked.

"Just do it."

Tony pulled the car to a halt on the curb. They left the vehicle.

"The tire tracks stop here, in front of tracks left by another truck," Tony observed.

"So they stopped the first truck here," Dale said.

"I see shoeprints in the mud," Dave suggested. "These were made by Melissa's shoes."

"Which obviously means," Dale decided, "they took Melissa from the first truck into the second truck and drove her into Lincoln."

"Where in Lincoln?" Tony asked.

"The only way to find out," Dale said, "is to search the whole area of Lincoln, following the second truck's tire tracks."

"Get in the car," Dave said. "I'll drive."

***

At Lincoln Clinic, in a spare room next to the main office, Melissa was lying on her side on a bed. This time, her hands were tied in front of her to the bed's rail overlooking the room, the strap tight around her wrists. She noticed her cellphone was no longer in her jeans pocket. At Montana Drive, the mobsters in the hallway must have overheard her calling Nicole, then Nicole telling her she would trace her GPS signal and contact Dave.

Melissa knew that, when she was led by Calvera, Batista and five men into the first truck, other men had stayed inside the building to booby-trap the place. She had smelt gasoline on the carpet and canisters of liquid fertilizer converted into explosives. Just like the fertilizer that blew up Ontario Drive. With a chill in her guts, she feared for the other FBI agents' safety.

Leaning upwards and glancing into the office, she spotted her cellphone on the desk. She had to untie herself. Biting the strap with her teeth, she loosened and snapped it.

At that moment, Doctor Rudy Kosinski opened the bedroom door and entered the room carrying a syringe full of cocaine.

"Hi, lady," he said. "My boss, Doctor Matt Detroit, will be here in a few seconds to oversee me executing you with an overdose of cocaine. But I see you've broken the strap we'd tied you up with. I will inject you now."

Kosinski charged toward the bed, raised the syringe and lunged for Melissa's right arm. But Melissa swerved out of the way and deflected his arm downward so the syringe accidentally stabbed into his leg. Melissa seized the lapels of Kosinski's jacket and, with a powerful head-butt, she smashed her forehead into his face. His nose exploded as blood gushed from his nostrils. But the burning agony in his face and the syringe jabbing into his leg failed to stop him. Kosinski grabbed her hair and wrenched her head back violently. Melissa's bare forehead creased up with the agony of her hair being pulled, and she cried out like a child. He ripped the syringe out of his leg, for no cocaine had been injected into this limb, but with a powerful self-defense move executed with deadly fury, Melissa slammed her hand into his nose, forcing the bridge into his brain. Kosinski coughed and choked as he died instantly and crumpled to the floor.

Climbing off the bed, Melissa ran for the office to retrieve her cellphone. But Doctor Matt Detroit ran through the bedroom door, seized her narrow shoulders and wrenched her toward him.

"Oh no you don't!" he growled.

Doctor Detroit tried to restrain Melissa in a grappling hold, but she bashed her bony elbow three times into his stomach. He doubled up in agony, releasing his hold on her. Trapping his arm in an armlock, she kneed him in the stomach, knocking all the wind out of him, before she threw two elbow strikes to his shoulder blade, hurling him to the floor.

On the desk, just inside the office, was a glass bottle of water. Melissa grabbed it. Still not defeated by Melissa's karate and self-defense moves, Doctor Detroit scrambled off the floor again, his large, strong hands reaching for her throat. But Melissa dodged aside and with savage force, she sent the bottle crashing down toward Detroit's head. The glass weapon smashed into two pieces. His brain was jarred by the blow so he crumpled to the floor, out cold.

Melissa gasped and gulped, inhaling and exhaling desperately. She kept hold of the top half of the broken bottle to use as a weapon in case Detroit went for her again. The sharp, jagged edges would cut him very severely, or even kill him.

Regaining her breath, she ran into the office and grabbed her cellphone. She turned it on and dialed Dale Manuchi's cell.

"Come on, come on, please," she whined. "Please answer me, Dale, honey."

But then Doctor Detroit's shadow closed in around her, the big brute clenching the syringe of cocaine in his large hand. Melissa screamed, her shrill shriek carrying through the bedroom door so it could be heard a hundred yards away. Detroit lunged downward with the syringe, but Melissa swerved again, the top half of the broken bottle still in her hand. He lost his footing and fell upon the windowsill. Taking her moment to act, Melissa stabbed the broken glass square into his throat, rupturing his windpipe, carotid artery and jugular vein. Screaming with agony, Detroit collapsed into a heap on the office floor, dying in a matter of seconds. His blood soaked Melissa's hands as she dropped the broken bottle.

Grabbing her cellphone, she fled out of the office and through the bedroom door. She turned a corner and sprinted into the next corridor, breathing and grunting in a distressed state, desperate to find a boiler room. This was the last place the security guards or Calvera's mobsters would look for her. Due to Calvera telling the other doctors and nurses that Melissa was a psychopath who had murdered one of his men, these care staff would view her as a threat to their safety rather than a scared, distressed woman terrified for her life. This was even more likely due to her self-defense killings of doctors Rudy Kosinski and Matt Detroit.

Nurses who discovered their corpses in the spare bedroom would not know they were hired by Calvera and Batista to kill Melissa and would be even more convinced she was a deranged woman the security guards must shoot to kill.

Melissa's only hiding place was the boiler room, and she speeded toward it. Just around the corner, in the corridor, she heard the five Cubans telling each other they must punish her for the two doctors' killings. The same Cubans who had held her captive at Montana Drive and been in the truck with Calvera. Now they were advancing down the corridor, bent on Melissa's murder. If they turned the corner, she would be spotted, and they would shoot her on sight. Frantically pulling open the door, she leaped into the boiler room, seized the door's key from a shelf and locked it.

Melissa hid in a corner and dialed Dale's cellphone number. It bleeped three times.

"Come on, come on, please," she whimpered. Tears flowed down her feminine face.

Then Dale answered the call.

"Hi there," he said. "Is that you, Melissa?"

"Yes, honey. I'm in trouble."

"Okay, calm down. Where are you?"

"At Lincoln Clinic in the town of Lincoln, Pennsylvania," Melissa said. "I escaped from two drug-dealing doctors working for Calvera, doctors who tried to kill me with an overdose of cocaine. Calvera's men are now combing the clinic, looking for me. I'm hiding in the clinic's boiler room."

"You're hiding in the boiler room!" Dale exclaimed. "You dumb bitch, Melissa! If Calvera's men find you, there's no escape!"

"Hey, don't call me a dumb bitch!" Melissa cried. "I'm not dumb! The boiler room is the last place Calvera's men will search. You three guys must drive over here fast!"

"I'll tell Dave. He's driving. Hang in there."

"Please hurry, honey," Melissa whimpered.

"We will."

Melissa hung up, breathing heavily with petrified terror.

***

Five minutes later, Timlook PD's civilian car raced to an abrupt stop in the clinic's car park, and Dave, Tony and Dale emerged from the vehicle. They sprinted toward the front entrance, then darted inside. The security guards obstructed them.

"You can't come in here," one guard said.

"We're FBI agents," Dave said. "Agents Bradley, Selma and Manuchi."

"These are our ID cards," Dale offered.

"Did any Cubans come in here?" Tony asked.

"Five Cubans," the guard said.

"They're about to commit a murder," Dave warned him. "A woman is in danger, and we must find her before they do. Where's the boiler room?"

"In the last corridor leading left from the end of that corridor to your right. You'll need assistance."

"No, we'll go alone," Dave said. "We have to run."

The three FBI agents turned left at the end of the corridor and spotted the five Cubans trying to force the boiler room's door. From overhearing Melissa's call to Dale, they had discovered her hiding place. Now, one mobster pointed his handgun inside the keyhole, ready to blast the lock. Once inside the cupboard, they would finish off Melissa for good. But Dave, Tony and Dale aimed their rifles toward the mobsters.

"Freeze, you bastards!" Dave shouted.

"Get down on the ground!" Tony yelled.

The Cubans raised their handguns, but the FBI agents opened fire with deadly fury. Dale blasted two mobsters with three rifle shots while Tony blazed two gunshots into the third guy. Three bursts of gunfire from Dave's rifle caught the last two brutes in the solar plexus and chest. Their jackets soaked with blood from their injuries, the Cubans fell to the concrete floor and died.

The agents hurried down the corridor toward the boiler room door, and Dave knocked.

"Are you there, Melissa?" he cried.

"It's us," Dale said. "It's safe to come out."

"We'd never let you down," Tony told her.

Melissa turned the key in the lock, replaced it on the shelf and then pushed the door open. Shaking her long hair back behind her shoulders, she bit her lip nervously, tears streaming from her eyes. Then she ran into Dale's arms, and he embraced her with all his strength, crushing her firmly against his chest.

"Thank God you're here," Melissa stammered. "Fuck, fuck and fucking hell. I thought I would never get out of this alive."

"Where are the two drug-dealing doctors who tried to kill you?" Dale asked.

"With an overdose of cocaine," Tony commented.

"Let me guess," Dave remarked, "you knocked them out with your karate and self-defense skills."

"I did more than that," Melissa replied. "I killed them. One with a hand strike to the nose and the other with a broken bottle to the throat. And I would do the same thing again. I also knew you three would never let me down."

"We wouldn't," Dale promised.

"You can count on that," Dave assured her.

Then the security guards jogged down the corridor.

"Everything okay?" one guy asked.

"Everything's okay," Dave reassured them. "Agent Melissa Morgan is safe now."

"Agent Melissa Morgan!" the guard exclaimed. "Calvera told us she's a dangerous psychopath who killed one of his men!"

"She's an FBI agent, and she's also my wife," Dale said.

"She's not a psychopath," Tony told the guards.

"I've killed several men in the line of duty," Melissa said. "Including some of Calvera's men because they peddle narcotics and arms. The two doctors I killed in the spare room near their office were on Calvera's payroll, and they almost injected an overdose of cocaine into me. But they bit off more than they could chew. My actions were justifiable self-defense."

"You mind if we call the Lincoln police over here?" the other guard asked. "So you can recount your whole story to the cops."

"You do that," Dave agreed.

"But before doing that," Melissa said, "I'm hungry and also thirsty. You mind if we all drop in at the clinic's cafe and buy some food and drinks?"

"You do that," the guard told them. "And we're all terribly sorry we believed Calvera's phony story that you were a psychopath."

"No shit." Melissa chuckled. "And no hard feelings." Her beaming grin reached both sides of her face.

***

In the cafe, the four FBI agents sat around a table eating sandwiches and drinking hot chocolate, coffee or lemonade. Dave and Tony were positioned opposite Dale and Melissa, and Dave noticed Dale crying.

"You look upset, Dale," he remarked. "What's wrong?"

"I almost lost Melissa," Dale said. "I nearly failed her, let her down. I'll never do that again." He wiped the tears from his face and beard.

Melissa gently took his shoulders in her hands and leaned toward his head. "Oh Dale, no. You would never fail me or let me down. Nor would Dave and Tony. I was scared, but you were there for me. And I would always protect you, Dave and Tony, as you would protect me. Don't feel guilty, my love." She kissed his mouth, her forehead pressed against his.

"We work as a team," Tony promised him.

"And we've all been there," Dave said. "A few days ago, we lost James Mitchell. I felt empty inside. Jim took too many bullets and died as a result. And I felt like I failed Jim, let him down. It's tough being a cop, but Jim died doing the job he loved doing. It could've been me who took too many bullets."

"Be grateful that you didn't," Tony advised him.

"Don't psychoanalyze yourself," Dale said. "You're right. We've all been there. I did it to myself just now. Beating myself up over what very nearly happened to Melissa."

"Dale," Melissa began hesitantly. "Do you really think I'm a dumb bitch?"

"Yes, I do. You're too emotional, you get scared too easily, and you lock yourself in a boiler room where five mobsters can easily corner you. Why didn't you run toward an open door or climb through a window? Then I wouldn't have to psychoanalyze myself about how I would cope if I lost you, the way Dave psychoanalyzed himself about losing Jim."

"I did the same, Dale," Tony objected. "Jim was a good cop. Didn't you?"

"I guess I did," Dale admitted. "I certainly did."

"You have every right to be mad at me, Dale," Melissa told him. "I was dumb. And I am too emotional and I get scared too easily. Being kidnapped makes you scared. But next time, I'll escape through a door or a window, not lock myself in a boiler room."

"Okay, I think it's time for us to go," Dave announced. "The cops are waiting for us."

**

The four FBI agents encountered the Lincoln cops in the car park outside the clinic. A police sergeant approached them.

"Are you FBI Agents Dave Bradley, Tony Selma, Dale Manuchi and Melissa Morgan?" he asked.

"We are, and we're from Timlook in western Pennsylvania," Tony said.

"You're under arrest for a series of murders down in Maryland," the sergeant declared. "At Chandler and Co. Business and the Timber Wolf Roadhouse, a massacre at the arms dealers' hideout, an explosion at Montana Drive and Melissa killing two doctors in self-defense. If you all cooperate and come with us, we won't put you in handcuffs. You're all deadly in the use of karate, kung fu and self-defense, but you're not dangerous cop-killers."

"All our actions were self-defense, not murder," Melissa told him.

"We'll justify ourselves at Lincoln PD," Dale suggested.

"Let's just go along quietly," Dave advised everybody. "And I mean quietly. That way, we won't end up in handcuffs."

***

At Lincoln PD, the FBI agents shared a prison cell, but Dave remained positive. Even though he could not call Nicole at Timlook PD due to the Lincoln cops confiscating the agents' cellphones, he would call her in an hour's time to inform her they had escaped from Calvera's gangs.

The Captain of Lincoln PD wandered down the corridor and turned toward the guard. "You mind opening the jail cell?"

"After they murdered so many criminals?"

"I said open the jail cell!" the captain shouted. "That's an order!"

The guard turned his key inside the lock and opened the cell door.

"You FBI Agents Dave Bradley, Tony Selma, Dale Manuchi and Melissa Morgan?" the captain asked.

"Yes, Captain, we are," Dave told him. "I run this team."

"My name's Captain Robert Delarno. You mind coming with me?"

There were four rigorous interrogations, each FBI agent being questioned separately. Dave was the first to be interrogated, during which he phoned Nicole at Timlook PD. Nicole told Captain Delarno that all four FBI agents were outstanding agents with clean records. Delarno thanked Nicole, and Dave explained the situation to him.

After the interrogations, the FBI agents were brought together inside the role-call room with the police officers who had questioned them.

"Okay, you four," Delarno began. "Are you familiar with the charges brought against you by Luis Calvera and Ramon Batista?"

"We are," Dave said.

"First of all, you and Agent Selma," Delarno continued. "At The Chandler and Co. Business, which sells trucks down in Maryland, the bodies of Robert Chandler and his five workers were found with injuries consistent with karate or kung fu blows or kicks. Forensics and CSI matched DNA samples to the DNA profiles of Agents Bradley and Selma on the police database.

"Then there was a massacre at the Timber Wolf Roadhouse outside Baltimore, before all four of you claim Calvera and Batista demolished the roadhouse with one of their trucks. Forensics saw the front wall bashed in. No DNA was found on the mobsters whom you shot and killed, and those who survived and were later arrested told us the four of you were shooting and killing their friends indiscriminately. But we found broken chairs in the bar area, indicating they threw chairs at you and you fired to defend yourselves. When Calvera and Batista rammed their truck through the wall, you all escaped through a window. Four men blocked your escape, and you shot them. As you drove away, two trucks pursued you, each truck having two men in the front seats. Each of you agents fired at the men; the bullets penetrated the windshields and killed them.

"Then there were two separate kidnappings. Agents Bradley, Selma and Manuchi were abducted from a saloon and held captive at a hideout somewhere in Maryland. Six Cubans were about to interrogate you, but you killed them with your karate and kung fu skills. Two mobsters were shot in the head with a handgun, which we later took from Bradley, along with the three rifles Bradley, Selma and Manuchi stole from the dead interrogators. As you three escaped from the hideout, you killed ten guards, then shot and killed four mobsters who fired at you. Your DNA was taken from the six interrogators in the mobsters' prison cell, and then the ballistics report at Baltimore PD traced the bullets inside the twenty mobsters to the handgun and the three rifles we took from you here at Lincoln PD.

"Added to this, Calvera's third hideout, Montana Drive, was destroyed in an explosion caused by a lit fire torch, gasoline on the carpet and canisters of liquid fertilizer transformed into explosives, like in the blast that destroyed Ontario Drive. You three claim it wasn't you who blew up Montana Drive. Calvera's mobsters booby-trapped Montana Drive in order to massacre you three, and you only ventured onto those premises because you believed Agent Melissa Morgan was being held captive there.

"Which brings me to the second kidnapping, of Agent Morgan. Morgan was held captive at Montana Drive, where she used her cellphone to contact Captain Nicole Lamenski at Timlook PD. Nicole traced Morgan's GPS signal to Montana Drive and then contacted Agent Bradley. Bradley, Selma and Manuchi drove to Montana Drive to rescue Morgan, but the Cubans had already taken her, in their truck, to Lincoln. Calvera and Batista and five Cubans told the doctors and nurses at Lincoln Clinic that Agent Morgan was a dangerous psychopath who had killed one of Calvera's men and she was not to be trusted. Two doctors named Rudy Kosinski and Matt Detroit tied her hands to her bed's rail and were about to inject an overdose of cocaine into her arm, which would kill her. We know the doctors were guilty because Forensics and CSI found the syringe with cocaine lying on the floor with their DNA all over it. But Melissa Morgan turned the tables on both doctors, using her karate and self-defense skills. She head-butted Kosinski and then bashed his nose into his brain before she fought with Detroit and stabbed him in the neck with a broken bottle. She retrieved her cellphone, escaped from the spare bedroom near Detroit's office, hid in a boiler room and called Agent Manuchi.

The five Cubans discovered the doctors' bodies, then searched the corridors for Agent Morgan. Due to overhearing her talking to Manuchi on her cellphone, they discovered her hiding place. They repeatedly forced the door, but it wouldn't open. One of them was about to shoot the lock, but Bradley, Selma and Manuchi arrived just in time. You three shouted at the mobsters, ordering them to drop their weapons and lie face down on the floor. The mobsters raised their handguns, but with your rifles, you shot and killed all five of them. Then Morgan came out of the boiler room, and you had lunch and drinks in the clinic's cafe before my uniforms arrested you. Do any of you have anything to add?"

"No, we don't," Dale said.

"Nor do I," Melissa said.

"I don't," Tony told Delarno.

"I have two questions," Dave said. "Will we be charged with all these self-defense killings, which make it seem like we were vigilante cops committing murders in revenge for the murder of FBI Agent James Mitchell? Calvera and Batista were responsible for Jim's death in that bank raid in Timlook. Will these self-defense killings lead to us being tried, convicted and sent to Death Row? And if not, may we continue to pursue this case to bring down Calvera, Batista and their mob?"

"Due to mitigating circumstances," Delarno explained, "like Jim's death, you agents acting in self-defense and you all being kidnapped, which meant that to escape your kidnappers you had to use extreme force—no, none of you will be tried, convicted or imprisoned. But you cannot continue to pursue this case against Calvera, Batista and their mobsters. It's out of your hands."

"Then what should we do?" Dave asked.

"Return to Timlook. We'll give you back your cellphones, your three rifles and the handgun you stole from the six Cubans who tried to interrogate you. Detective Morgan will keep the handgun on her. You'll also have your civilian car back, and as you drive back to Timlook, I'll have four squad cars escort you through eastern Pennsylvania. Just in case you have ideas about pulling another operation against Calvera and Batista."

"That's rather extreme," Tony said.

"Jim's death will be for nothing," Dale remarked.

"Who else will bring down Calvera and Batista if we don't?" Dave asked.

"Nobody can," Delarno told them. "They are untouchables. And due to the number of mobsters you've all killed, Calvera and Batista can throw just as many charges against you as you can against them. The courts will see you as vigilantes, as maverick cops, the strongest charge against you being murder on a scale you would only expect from a serial killer. And most of Calvera and Batista's arms-dealing activities have been within the law. Even if we can nail both dealers and their mob, convict them for arms and drug dealing, money laundering, kidnapping and a whole series of murders in Florida, Maryland and Pennsylvania, they cannot go down for life on Death Row without dragging you four down with them, because you killed as many of them as they killed cops and civilians, and the courts won't see you as exercising justice but exercising revenge and murder. If you want to continue upholding the law, walk away from all this now. Four squad cars will escort you back to Timlook."

"Can we take one last look at your police intranet and DNA database?" Dave wanted to know.

"To what end?" Delarno asked.

"Firstly, to prove the mobsters we killed can be linked to Calvera and Batista," Dave said. "And secondly, the serial numbers on the weapons you confiscated from these mobsters will trace these weapons back to Calvera and Batista."

"That won't bring down their mob," Delarno decided. "But we may come up with something new in this case."

Delarno and two uniformed cops escorted the FBI agents into the computer room. They browsed through the intranet and DNA databases with a fine-tooth comb.

"You're right," Delarno said. "All these weapons have only one source: The Cuban mob run by Luis Calvera and Ramon Batista. And the mobsters' DNA links these guys only to one mob. Calvera's mob."

"So we have something on these guys," Melissa said.

"We can build another case," Dale told Delarno.

"And arrange to have immunity from prosecution," Tony suggested.

"All we need to do is cut a deal with the courts," Dave told the other three agents.

"That way, Calvera and Batista can't drag us down for exercising retribution against their mob."

"It ain't that simple," Delarno blurted. "Calvera and Batista's arms-dealing activities were within the law. In a gun culture like America, arms dealing is as legal as buying or selling weapons from a gun store, whether arms dealers sell weapons to other countries, terrorist groups, or drug cartels in South America, or they buy or sell weapons within our borders. Even if we nail the mobsters on charges of drug dealing, money laundering and a whole series of murders, we can't nail them for arms dealing. On top of all this, Calvera and Batista still have a mob of over thirty tough guys fully armed with the most terrifying weapons, and the most dangerous mob in Maryland and Pennsylvania. Even my guys and the SWAT teams are too scared to take them on. Not without losing several men and women in the process. If you want to stay alive, and avoid rotting in prison cells on Death Row, walk away from all this. Walk away. And get Captain Nicole Lamenski to pay you a handsome sum of money to pay your bills."

"We have no choice," Dave agreed. "We'll leave Lincoln."

***

Four squad cars surrounded Timlook PD's civilian car. Dave and Tony climbed into the front seats, with Tony driving, whilst Dale and Melissa lowered themselves into the back seats. The three rifles were situated on the floor in front of the back seats, whilst Melissa placed the handgun she had confiscated beside the rifles. Her lips met Dale's beard with a gentle kiss. Dave rubbed his beard while Tony caressed his moustache and straightened his glasses. He keyed the civilian car's ignition and began driving.

With two squad cars in front and the other two behind, Dave knew there was no way Timlook PD's civilian car would escape from this net of police vehicles.

"They gave us our weapons back," Tony told Dave, "and also our cellphones."

"Which reminds me," Dave said, "I must call Nicole."

"You go ahead."

Dave unlocked his phone and dialed Nicole's number. There were three bleeps before Nicole answered.

"Hi, Captain Nicole Lamenski at Timlook PD responding. Is that you, Dave?"

"It's me," Dave said. "How are you, honey?"

"I'm fine, honey. Because you were at Lincoln PD, I hatched on that you four had escaped from being held captive by the arms trafficking gangs. Is Melissa safe? And are Dale and Tony safe? I hear the engine of our civilian car droning in the background."

"It is the civilian car we're driving," Dave replied. "Tony is driving. Tony, Dale and I escaped from our captors, and then we rescued Melissa. But we were arrested by the Lincoln police and ruthlessly interrogated about the vast number of mobsters we all killed. Captain Robert Delarno took into account mitigating circumstances and how we all acted in self-defense, and he released us. But he told us we have no case against Calvera and Batista's mob. The courts will rule that we killed as many mobsters as they killed cops and civilians. If they go down for life on Death Row, they'll drag us down with them. And I doubt if we can plead to the courts to give us immunity from prosecution. So Captain Delarno has sent us driving back to Timlook, with four squad cars in front and behind us, so we can't escape. We have no case against Calvera and Batista."

"I'm sorry, honey," Nicole told Dave. "You must be really pissed off. And you must feel you failed Jim."

"I did fail Jim," Dave growled. "But Jim's death won't go unpunished. We'll find other ways to nail the mobsters. But my cellphone is running out of credit. I have to go now, Nicole. I send you my love."

Dave and Nicole bade each other farewell and cut off contact.

"You feel pissed off, huh?" Tony asked.

"I do," Dave said.

"We're all pissed off. Not just you."

"When up against brutal scum like Calvera and Batista, the worst thing we can do is give up!" Dave cried.

"Hey, calm down!" Tony shouted. "I know you, Dave. I've only known you for a few months, but Jim, Dale and Melissa have known you for many years. You're like Jim. Jim never gave up. And you never give up.

When we return to Timlook, we'll find other ways to bring down Calvera and Batista."

"It ain't that easy! Delarno was right: Calvera and Batista are untouchables."

"We'll think of something, Dave," Melissa promised him. "There's always a way to bring down bastards like Calvera and Batista if we persevere. I'm sure all young detectives would want to be as committed, determined and effective as you. Don't you think there's still hope, Dale, honey?"

"There is hope," he assured her. "Where there's a will, there's a way. And you're right, Melissa. All young detectives would want to be as determined and effective as Dave and Tony. And you, too. You were always a good cop: strong, brave and determined. Although you are too emotional and get scared too easily, you've fought your fear many times. It's an honor to have you as a sidekick to back me up, and also back up Dave and Tony. Behind every strong man is a strong woman."

"You're as wise as me," Melissa chuckled. "Thanks, my love." She leaned over and kissed him repeatedly on the mouth. Dale kissed her forehead twice before her hand swept back her shoulder-length hair.

Then she heard the sound of propellers above the civilian car. "What's that?" she asked. "That sounds like a helicopter. Do you hear it, guys?"

"I hear it!" Dave shouted. "It is a helicopter! That's a bad sign!"

"A bad sign?!" Dale cried. "How do you mean?"

"Stay calm," Melissa begged him. "Tony, young man, drive our car into the field of long grass, so we can hide from the helicopter."

"Hide from the helicopter?!" Tony exclaimed.

"We're about to come under attack," Dave said. "Drive into the field, now. Jump to it."

"Okay, okay."

Tony swerved, and the car leaped down the embankment into the field and disappeared amongst the long, five-foot-tall grass. The four squad cars careered to a halt, but this was the uniformed cops' worst mistake. The helicopter speeding above fired a volley of rockets which ploughed savagely into the vehicles. A series of ferocious blasts ripped across the country road, transforming all the squad cars into orangey-yellow fireballs, sending black smoke billowing a hundred yards or more. Dave, Tony, Dale and Melissa scrambled out of the civilian car and were struck with blind horror and terror.

"Calvera and Batista sent that helicopter," Melissa said.

"You think so?" Dale asked.

"She knows so," Tony corrected him.

"And the helicopter is coming back," Dave whispered.

"We need to get our rifles!" Dale cried.

"And hurry up," Melissa pleaded. "I'll use the handgun."

They ran back toward the car and grabbed their guns. All four took aim. The helicopter was only three hundred yards away and was closing in on the FBI agents with tremendous speed. Melissa squeezed the handgun's trigger, but the weapon jammed.

"Damn it, no!" She dived into the grass. She quickly fixed the gun's magazine, but Dave, Tony and Dale were already blasting at the helicopter.

Tony and Dale blazed fifteen rifle shots through the windshield, killing the three bearded Cubans inside the cockpit. Dave pumped five shots into the fuel tank.

The burning hot bullets and the sparks circulating around the ruptured tank ignited the fuel. Three seconds later, the helicopter exploded with a savage blast that thundered through the air, sending balls of fire and smoke as well as metal, glass and propellers flying everywhere.

"Get down!" Dave shouted.

All four FBI agents dropped face down onto the embankment, narrowly missing the shards of metal and glass.

"That was close!" Tony cried.

"Too right it was," Dale said.

"My handgun jammed!" Melissa cried.

"Have you fixed it?" Dale asked.

"I've fixed the magazine."

"It should work now," Dale decided.

"It's too late for that," Dave said.

"The helicopter is down," Tony told them.

"One question," Dale said.

"Carry on, honey," Melissa suggested.

"Are more mobsters coming after us? And if so, how many more?"

"More than thirty," Dave informed him.

"Either in helicopters or trucks," Tony added.

"More like trucks," Dave told him.

"How do you know they'll travel in trucks, not helicopters?"

"Trucks can carry more men. Calvera and Batista will send a few trucks down this highway to pursue us. Or probably cover many highways. In the meantime, we brought changes of clothes with us in our small cases. We must use the cover of this long grass to strip naked, then put on fresh clothes. Including jeans, socks, underwear and cooler shirts. Not these denim shirts."

"Are you happy for us to see your naked body, Melissa?" Dale asked.

"I'm not that kind of girl," Melissa objected. "We don't yet smell of sweat, but I need a fresh pair of jeans and a cooler shirt."

"We must have showers long before we reach Timlook," Dave said.

"Can you think of anywhere we can stop off?" Tony asked him.

"Lancaster County, a few miles west of Philadelphia," Dale cut in.

"That's what I was thinking," Dave said. "The domain of the Amish people."

"The Amish people!" Dale exclaimed.

"Why not your Quaker family, the Bradleys, who live in that Quaker hamlet?" Melissa asked.

"We'll stop off at my sister Rachel's farmstead between Philadelphia and Lancaster

County," Dave continued. "Only Rachel lives in the Quaker hamlet. My father Jacob and mother Rebecca died a few years ago. My father in 2016, and my mother in 2018. But my sister Rachel is aged forty now. She runs the Quaker hamlet, the church and the farms on her own. The other two Quaker families at the hamlet have left, but she keeps all three houses in brilliant condition."

"I'm sorry your parents died," Tony said.

"Thanks for the sympathy, but I'm okay," Dave replied. "When we've wiped out Calvera's mob, we'll drop by Rachel's farmstead."

"It's best we give her our sympathy," Tony suggested.

"We will," Dave agreed. "If we survive our last battle with Calvera and Batista's mobsters, who have us heavily outnumbered and outgunned. But I have a plan."

***

While the four FBI agents were naked and hidden in the grass, they covered themselves with shampoo, poured big bottles of cool water over themselves and then dried themselves with towels. Then they put on changes of jeans, socks, underwear and shirts. Dave and Tony wore blue shirts whilst Dale's top was white, and Melissa was dressed in a pink shirt. She kissed Dale.

"Did you enjoy being naked?" Dale asked.

"No, I did not," Melissa chuckled.

"None of us did," Tony said. "But nobody in any passing cars saw us. We must drive the civilian car back up the embankment."

"That will be extremely difficult," Dave said. "But the embankment leads up to that side road over there, cutting off from the highway. We'll drive fast through the mud and grass so we don't get stuck in the mud, and then we'll double back along the side road until we come back onto the highway."

"Where do we stop for dinner?" Melissa said.

"There's bound to be a diner, a roadhouse or a saloon somewhere," Dave promised her.

"Good, because I'm hungry," Dale said. "And so is Melissa."

"I'm hungry too," Tony cut in.

"One thing at a time, guys," Dave insisted.

"Filling our bellies must be our first priority," Tony suggested. "And then we'll have the strength to take on Calvera's mobsters."

"We can wait another hour before we eat," Dale told him.

"I guess I can wait that long." Melissa sighed. "As long as it's only another hour."

"Thanks for the consideration," Dave said. "I'll find somewhere to eat in a nearby town or village."

After speeding through the field of long grass, the civilian car careered onto the side road before the vehicle drove slowly toward the highway. Now taking over the driving from Tony, Dave took the turn and accelerated toward Lancaster County.

"You know what?" Tony began.

"What are you thinking?" Dale asked.

"This vehicle feels pretty beaten up." Melissa chuckled.

"It's not that! The fuel gauge is running low. We need more fuel."

"I'll find a fuel station," Dave said.

They arrived at a Shell gas station, and Dave drove slowly between two fuel pumps containing unleaded gasoline.

"One question, Dave," Tony began.

"Go on," Dale said.

"He was asking Dave!" Melissa cried.

"Okay, stop arguing," Dave ordered. He addressed Tony. "Out with the question, young man."

"Is this car ozone-friendly?" Tony asked. "Does it run on unleaded fuel, which doesn't pollute the atmosphere and erode the ozone layer?"

"You think Timlook PD doesn't care about the environment?" Dave snapped. "And green issues? Of course it's ozone-friendly! All of Timlook's cars and vehicles are ozone-friendly! Virginia, Maryland and Pennsylvania want to set a green example to the rest of America, starting with their vehicles! Maryland and Pennsylvania pride themselves on liberal values as much as the rest of New England. And a Quaker like me first introduced my wife Nicole to green energy and green vehicles. Like this civilian car. Now can I fill the gasoline tank or will you?"

"I will," Tony said. "You didn't have to shout my head off. I get the message."

He opened the fuel tank before taking the pipe from the fuel pumps and wedging it into the tank.

"Another question," Dale said.

"How much fuel?" Melissa asked.

"Stop now," Dave demanded. "That's enough fuel."

***

The civilian car speeded through the rolling fields, pastures and meadows of Pennsylvania, then the forests and woods of deciduous trees with thick trunks and broad leaves. The deciduous trees varied in color from red, orange, yellow and brown to several shades of green.

"This countryside is so beautiful," Tony said.

"You bet it is," Dale agreed. "You bet."

"Can we all sing a song?" Melissa suggested cheerily. "Row, row, row the boat, gently down the stream, merrily, merrily, merrily, merrily…

"Oh, what's the next line? Come on, what's the next line? I really hate singing by myself and making a fool of myself. What about 'One man went to mow'? One man went to mow, went to mow a meadow, one man, two men, three men and their dog, went to mow a meadow…"

"You sound drunk." Tony laughed.

"I sound drunk?" Melissa giggled. "That's rich coming from you. How many times have you got drunk?"

"I don't know. More times than you. I stand corrected."

"There you go." Dale chuckled. "The buck stops with you."

"Okay, listen, guys, ladies," Dave called back.

"We're listening," Tony said.

"We're nowhere near any city, town or village," Dave told them. "But ahead of us, I see a restaurant in the middle of the countryside. I'm about to pull in, and we'll all order different meals of our choice. Avoid drinking alcohol because we may need to take turns to drive. We'll have starters and main meals, but no puddings. The sooner we leave, find a lay-by and then sleep inside this civilian car, the more refreshed we will be in the morning. Calvera and Batista's mobsters don't know we've stopped here. But somewhere out in the open, we'll set a trap for those mobsters and take them down. And then we'll make our way toward Philadelphia and then Lancaster County."

"Wait a minute, Dave!" Dale exclaimed. "Are you saying we'll take down over thirty mobsters with only four of us?"

"Yes, he is, honey," Melissa confirmed Dave's plan. "Never underestimate Dave

Bradley. Like his deceased partner, Jim, Dave is full of cunning ideas to bring down ruthless mobs even as evil and brutal as Calvera and Batista's. Numbers are not everything. It's brains over brawn, and Dave has both."

"Dave is full of surprises," Tony told them. "And so am I."

"But it will require careful planning," Dave said. "We're in the restaurant's car park now. First, we'll eat. Then we'll spend the night sleeping in this car until early in the morning, round about six a.m. We'll find another fuel station. Not to buy gasoline, but to buy sausage rolls, meat pies and muffins, together with bottles of drink for our breakfast. Then we'll rehearse our plan again and again. This plan will wipe out Calvera and Batista's mob."

"You are ambitious." Tony chuckled. "I'll give you that. I like your attitude."

***

Inside the restaurant's bar area, sitting around an enormous table, the FBI agents dined on four small starters before consuming four big meals, their plates overflowing with food.

As Dave suggested, they avoided alcoholic drinks. Melissa drank a lemonade while Dale and Dave consumed two large Pepsis and Tony guzzled down a glass of fizzy orange. Then they paid a fortune for their meals and drinks, each FBI agent pulling dollar bills out of their wallets.

Dave turned to the other three agents. "Did you all enjoy your meals?"

"Yeah, we did," Dale told him.

"I did too," Melissa enthused. "The best chicken in Pennsylvania."

"What about the French fries and vegetables?" Tony asked.

"The French fries and vegetables were beautiful." Melissa chuckled. "But the chicken was better."

"My steak, fries and vegetables were the best in Pennsylvania," Tony remarked.

"And so was my breaded fish stuffed with prawns and shrimps on a bed of rice and cabbage," Dale agreed.

"About my meal, guys," Dave told them. "My vegetable and mushroom lasagna mixed with carrots and turnips was the works. And now the waiter's coming." Dave passed him the money. "I'll pay nearly five dollars above the price. Keep the change."

***

In a lay-by in the forest, inside the car, the FBI agents slept until between 6 and 7 a.m. Dave woke up at 6:10 a.m., and the others awoke in the next twenty minutes.

"I slept like a dormant volcano," Dave said.

"So did I," Tony agreed.

"How was your sleep?" Melissa asked Dale.

"I had a bad dream," he replied.

"A bad dream?" Dave repeated. "I'm sorry. What was this dream?"

"It's really uncanny," Dale explained. "I was on a mountain ledge in Wyoming, looking down at the river below. Then I was in a serious predicament. A hungry grizzly bear sneaked up behind me, got his claws around my neck and shook me violently. The grizzly bear roared the most terrifying roaring, which petrified me more than a hurricane or an avalanche, and I thought my neck was going to break. Then there was darkness, and I woke up."

"There are no grizzlies in Pennsylvania," Melissa reassured him. "And no avalanches, except in the Appalachians."

"There are hurricanes," Tony told him.

"Oh, don't scare me," Dale pleaded. "An enormous bear with huge claws and massive fangs is scary enough."

"Snap out of it," Tony said.

"Nicole will have started work now at Timlook PD," Dave began. "I'll call her cellphone and ask for some information those eight bank raiders left behind when Jim and I killed them."

Dave made the call, and after a few bleeps, Nicole's voice sounded.

"Dave, is that you?"

"It is me," he replied. "Did you sleep well?"

"Yes, I did."

"How is everybody at Timlook PD?"

"They are fine," she explained. "Are you, Tony, Dale and Melissa okay?"

"We couldn't complain. Being a cop is tough, but then it always has been."

"Tell me about it."

"I was thinking about those eight bank raiders who died trying to rob the National Pennsylvania Bank," Dave said.

"They left evidence behind," Tony decided. He was definite.

"Thank you, Tony," Dave laughed. He addressed Nicole again. "Other cops at Timlook PD would've confiscated their cellphones. On their phones would be Luis Calvera's cellphone number, which they would text in order to maintain contact with Calvera. Are their cellphones nearby?"

"Yes, they are," Nicole told him. "In the evidence locker. I'll go there now to read Calvera's number and repeat it back to you. But one question? Why do you need Calvera's cellphone number? Calvera's mob is impossible to track down even on their mobiles, and they won't hang around in one place for more than a few minutes. Especially after Ontario Drive, the Timber Wolf Roadhouse and Montana Drive were destroyed, and they have no other hideout in Pennsylvania. The chances are they'll hang about in hotels or fly back to Cuba or South America. Why are you asking for Calvera's number now?"

"I intend to call him, and lure him into a trap," Dave told her. "Calvera, Batista and their whole gang of thirty to forty mobsters.

"Four of us can hide from these mobsters, while a whole squad of armed cops would be too conspicuous and would panic Calvera and his mob. We will have no backup, and we'll be seriously outnumbered. But we may be able to take down Calvera, Batista and their entire mob without having to use our weapons. The four of us cannot win against thirty or more mobsters in a shootout, but I've found another way to wipe out this whole private army."

"Being outnumbered, you four are taking an extremely dangerous risk," Nicole said. "If you don't use your rifles and handgun, how do you plan to kill over thirty guys?"

"Let me worry about that," Dave said. "Just read me Calvera's cellphone number when you've opened the evidence locker and checked Calvera and Batista's numbers on the bank raiders' phones."

"I've opened the locker now," Nicole told him. "Your cellphone can't text another person's phone, but you can call them on this number. On the eight bank raiders' phones, Calvera's number is exactly the same. You have a pen and paper?"

"Inside the car's glove compartment," Dave said. He opened the compartment, produced the pen and paper, and prepared to write. "I'm ready. What's the number?"

Nicole gave him the number. "You got that?"

"I got it," Dave confirmed. "Thanks, Nicole."

"Just one request from me," Nicole said.

"What is it, honey?"

"Please be careful, Dave, honey. I still haven't overcome the trauma of losing Jim. I don't want you four to end up the way Jim did."

"We'll be careful," Dave promised her. "I have to go now. Goodbye, Nicole."

They ended the call, and he turned toward the other FBI agents.

"That was a long call," Dale said.

"Do you have enough credit on your cellphone?" Melissa asked. "Or do you have to add more?"

"You can borrow one of our phones," Tony told him.

"There's still credit on my phone," Dave explained. "But before I call Calvera's number, we must stop off at a gas station to buy sausage rolls, meat pies and muffins for our breakfast. And drinks too, soft drinks or fruit juices. We'll all think and focus much better on full stomachs."

"That's cool." Dale laughed.

"I'm all for that, Dave." Melissa chuckled.

After eating pies and drinking a lemonade, an orange juice and two apple juices between them, the FBI agents drove toward Lake Jacob thirty miles south of Philadelphia. Then Dave stopped the car and addressed Tony, Dale and Melissa.

"There's a problem."

"A problem?" Melissa asked.

"What kind of a problem?" Dale wanted to know.

"My cellphone cannot show video of anybody receiving my call," Dave explained. "Nor can Tony or Melissa's. But Dale's phone can show Calvera and Batista as Calvera receives my call. It can also show us his license plate."

"His license plate!" Dale exclaimed.

"I know what you're planning," Melissa said.

"When you've filmed his license plate, Philadelphia PD can run an APB on his vehicle and track him down," Tony realized.

"What if he abandons his vehicle?" Dale asked.

"That's highly unlikely," Dave pointed out. "He needs a truck to carry at least ten men, something he can't do with a car or a jeep."

"You have a point," Tony said.

"I'm dying to hear more," Melissa enthused.

"You'll use his license plate to blackmail him?" Tony asked. "Giving him a reason to come all the way here to Lake Jacob to massacre us? Very neat."

"When I talk to and record Calvera and his truck's license plate, you, Tony, must write it down on this pad," Dave explained. "Here's the paper and pen."

Then Dave took Dale's cellphone and dialed Calvera's number. After a few bleeps, Calvera answered.

"Hi there, Luis Calvera answering your call," he replied. "It's you, Dave Bradley and Tony Selma. I see you on my cellphone."

"You're going to regret how you murdered my partner, Jim," Dave growled.

"Only four of you, planning to take down thirty-eight of us Cubans," Calvera said. "Including thirty mobsters in three trucks, and eight guys including Batista and myself in our eight-seater jeep."

The Cubans laughed.

"There will only be four of us taking you on," Dave agreed. "A whole squad of armed cops would be too conspicuous to you guys and would send you driving off. But four of us can pick off your men in a game of cat and mouse."

"And there's something else," Tony cut in. "I've just written down the license plates on all three trucks, so Philadelphia PD can run APBs on these vehicles and send squads of armed cops and FBI agents closing in on you."

"You low-down piece of scum, Bradley!" Calvera snarled.

"You're not laughing now," Dave growled. "If you want to destroy the evidence on Dale's cellphone, come and get us. We're at Lake Jacob thirty miles south of Philadelphia."

"We're coming for you!" Calvera cried and hung up.

Dave returned the cellphone to Dale.

"These are the license plates," Tony told Dave.

**

On a road overlooking Lake Jacob, the FBI agents spotted the eight-seater jeep leading the three trucks toward the lake, from a distance of eight hundred yards away.

"We're doing the really dangerous part," Dale told Melissa. "We'll shoot at the trucks' gasoline tanks, causing each truck to leak gasoline, and then shoot the trail of fuel to ignite it."

"Please be careful, Dale, honey," Melissa pleaded.

"We will," Dave promised her.

"You need to shoot at Calvera's eight-seater jecp, killing the two men sitting in the front," Dale explained. "Then shoot at the tire closest to the lake, so the jeep will swerve into the lake. A combination of drowning and hypothermia will kill the other six men, including Calvera and Batista."

Dale gently kissed Melissa's forehead, and she nodded that she understood.

"We'll hide in the grass," Dave whispered.

"Get ready, guys," Tony said.

Dave, Tony and Dale lay low in the long grass, and the eight-seater jeep closed in. When it was a hundred yards away, Melissa leaped into the road, stood with her legs apart and, with both hands, aimed her handgun at the driver and the man sat next to him. The men were startled, but Melissa pulled the trigger and blazed three shots into the driver. His chest bloodied and his head spilling blood, the bearded brute slumped onto the steering wheel. Melissa fired two gunshots into the other Cuban. Both bullets slammed violently through his head. He jerked backward and fell against the side door, blood gushing down his face and moustache. The jeep speeded toward Melissa, but she fired a shot into the wheel closest to the lake, puncturing the tire. The jeep swerved, flew above the embankment and crashed with brutal fury and terrifying impact into the lake before rolling upside down. Melissa was certain Calvera, Batista and the other bearded thugs in that jeep would never survive such a horrific accident, all six men dying from drowning and hypothermia whilst being trapped by their seatbelts in their seats underwater.

The remaining three trucks accelerated, but by then she was running away, sprinting down the side road. Melissa knew she would never outrun these trucks as the driver of the first truck was determined to run her over, but being a hundred yards in front, she could still run for long enough for Dave, Tony and Dale to fire three rifle shots into the trucks' gasoline tanks. They were ten yards apart, lying in the grass. They all fired at the same time. Dave's shot ruptured the first truck's gasoline tank while Tony's hit the second and Dale's gunshot slammed into the third truck's fuel tank. Three spurts of fuel gushed out of the tanks and soaked the road before Dave ignited the first trail of fuel with a shot from his rifle. Tony and Dale fired two shots into the other two trails of fuel, and three sets of flames lit up and speeded along all three trails of fuel. Melissa leaped into the grass.

She dropped onto her knees and rolled onto her front, hidden in the long grass as her blue jeans and pink shirt were roughed up by the impact of falling and rolling. The three trucks slammed to a halt, tires screeching against the road, before the thirty bearded and moustached Cubans with high-caliber rifles prepared to jump out. As Dave, Tony and Dale rejoined Melissa, the FBI agents took cover behind the embankment with their backs to the lake before the trails of fire reached the trucks' fuel tanks. A moment later, three savage blasts ripped the trucks to twisted, burning, smoldering metal, canvas and mutilated wheels, and all the Cubans inside perished in ferocious balls of flames and black smoke.

Glass and metal flew over the agents' heads as they pressed their bodies tight against the embankment, and then this dreaded hail stopped. The FBI agents climbed up the embankment, careful to avoid the pieces of broken glass, before they walked casually toward the dismembered, burning trucks and the criminals' mutilated corpses lying scattered across the road. These brutes were the last mobsters in Calvera's gang of arms traffickers.

"Whoa, whoa!" Melissa screamed with joy. "We did it! It worked! Your plan worked, Dave!"

"Our plan worked!" Dave shouted.

"We were all in this together!" Dale screamed.

Melissa threw her wiry arms around his neck and kissed him violently.

"All of us!" she cried. "Are you proud of me, Dave and Dale?"

"We're all proud of you," Dale growled.

"For popping those two drivers and then firing a gunshot into the tire," Tony said.

"Those shots were bang on target," Dale explained.

"Too right they were," Dave pointed out. "But then, Melissa was always a sharpshooter with a handgun or revolver."

"You can say that again." Tony chuckled.

"We all were great shots," Dave remarked. "Shooting those fuel tanks took expertise with rifles."

"You can't miss with a rifle," Tony explained. "Especially rifles as accurate as these. But now, we must search the area of water around the upside-down jeep in Lake Jacob."

"Why, Tony?" Dave asked.

"To make sure those six men, including Calvera and Batista really are dead."

"They will be," Dave promised everybody. "Now we must get into our car and drive toward Lancaster County. And visit the Quaker hamlet run by my sister Rachel."

As the car made its way north, six men swam from the upside-down jeep toward the bank and climbed out of the lake, freezing from the water soaking their jeans, shirts and leather jackets. Luis Calvera and Ramon Batista were among the gang. They were shocked and appalled when they saw the burning trucks and the mass of Cubans lying across the road.

"We lost our whole mob," Calvera snarled. "The last thirty men in our gang."

"We have no transport," Batista growled. "We must hire a car to take all six of us to Lancaster County."

"That's where Bradley's people are heading," Calvera hissed.

Outside Lancaster County, Melissa was driving the civilian car whilst Dale sat beside her and Dave and Tony were in the back seats.

"One thing I must mention," Dave began. "Due to Rachel being a Quaker who frowns upon violence, we must not mention our self-defense killings of Calvera and Batista's guys in Maryland and here in Pennsylvania. You got that?"

"We got it," Dale added.

"One thing," Melissa pointed out. "Can we have showers?"

"Yeah, you can," Dave replied. "She'll also cook us meals."

"I can't wait to eat her food," Melissa enthused.

She drove the car from the highway into the side road leading toward the Quaker hamlet. She stopped the vehicle beside Rachel's car and switched off the ignition. All four FBI agents pushed open the doors and climbed outside, and Dave pressed Rachel's doorbell.

"Who is it?" Rachel called.

"It's your big brother Dave! And my partner, FBI Agent Tony Selma, along with Agents Dale Manuchi and Melissa Morgan. We're all FBI agents now."

Rachel came to the front door and pulled it open. Although she was forty, she looked in her early thirties.

"Dave! Long time no see. You've all aged well and still look young. So you're FBI agents now? And who's this young man with blond hair, a moustache and glasses?"

"I'm FBI Agent Tony Selma."

"Dave and Dale, you've grown beards," Rachel pointed out. "But you still look quite young."

"You look young too," Dale complimented her. "Even though you've reached forty."

"Dale, no," Melissa chuckled. "You don't have to comment on her age."

"I'm sorry, ladies," Dale said, his voice friendly.

"It's okay," Rachel replied.

"These three houses look so clean and tidy," Dave pointed out.

"You reckon so?" Rachel asked.

"I know so."

"It's hard work keeping them clean," Rachel explained. "But it keeps me busy. I have a question?"

"A question?" Tony responded.

"Ask away," Dave invited her.

"Where is your wife, Nicole, and your old partner, Jim?"

"Nicole is now Captain of Timlook PD, and it's a very demanding job. She's doing well. But the news about Jim is not good. He was killed in the line of duty. Jim and I were staking out the National Pennsylvania Bank in Timlook when eight bank raiders rammed their truck through the wall and we got into a shootout with them. Jim shot and killed five of them whilst I shot three, but before these three men died, they shot and killed Jim. Everybody was upset and traumatized by Jim's death, most of all me. I had known Jim for twenty-six years, since the Klaus Rheitag case, and I always knew Jim had nine lives like a cat. But in that bank raid, Jim's luck ran out and he died in the shootout. Nicole is as upset as me, and everybody else at Timlook PD and the FBI."

"Oh, I'm sorry," Rachel groaned. "I always saw a perfect friend in Jim. I don't know what to say, except that I'm as upset and traumatized as all of you."

"We're dealing with it okay," Dave promised her.

"We offer you our sympathy over the deaths of your mother and father," Tony said. "Dave, Dale and Melissa knew about your parents' deaths, but I knew nothing. Until Dave told me when we were driving from Maryland back into Pennsylvania."

"You were in Maryland!" Rachel exclaimed. "What were you doing there?"

"I can't keep it a secret," Dave responded.

"Are you sure you want to tell her?" Tony asked.

"I must," Dave said, and then, "We were avenging Jim's murder. The bank raiders who killed Jim at the National Pennsylvania Bank were working for two Cuban arms dealers, Luis Calvera and Ramon Batista.

Us FBI agents couldn't persuade law enforcement in Maryland and Pennsylvania to bring down Calvera's mob, ready for legal prosecution. The mobsters numbered over fifty men armed with high-velocity rifles. The cops would've suffered heavy casualties in any planned operation against them. So we took the law into our own hands. After a few shootouts together with us using karate, kung fu and self-defense techniques, and then igniting the fuel tanks of three trucks containing thirty mobsters, we wiped out the entire mob."

"Calvera and Batista died by drowning," Tony remarked. "When their jeep flew off the road into Lake Jacob."

"Don't worry, all of you," Rachel replied. "It goes with the territory. Quaker or no Quaker, being a cop is a tough game."

"I always thought pigs would have wings before a Quaker became a cop," Tony said. "Until I met Dave."

"One question?" Dave asked Rachel. "Can the four of us have baths or showers in those three buildings, including your place? We've had a long journey from Maryland, and we need to clean ourselves up."

"Please, feel free."

***

After the four FBI agents had showered, they reconvened in Rachel's house.

"This is a spotless place," Dale praised her.

"You Quakers are like the Amish," Melissa added. "You keep your houses spotlessly clean."

"You think so?" Rachel asked.

"We know so," Dale said. "The Quakers are a Puritan people without being intolerant and imposing their faith on other people."

"The Amish are the same," Tony explained. "And they don't stress themselves out with the rat race the way us English do."

"You English?" Rachel said. "That's what the Amish call you white Americans. That's not what Quakers like me call you. Just call yourselves Americans. I must tell you something."

"Carry on, sister," Dave prompted her.

"I only have enough food in my place to feed myself," Rachel told them. "With my parents gone and the other two Quaker families having left for Philadelphia, I can't raise farm animals or grow vegetable or fruit crops on my own. I either buy my food from the chain stores in Philadelphia or collect surplus food from the Amish communities in Lancaster County. But I can run you over to Philadelphia in my car so you can all buy takeout."

Everybody nodded their heads in agreement.

"Chinese or Italian?" asked Dave.

Taking Timlook PD's car and Rachel's car, they drove to a Chinese restaurant. All four agents and Rachel bought five dishes and five containers of rice. They waited for their orders.

"It's a long time since we've had Chinese," Dave pointed out.

"You were always the health food fanatic," Rachel said. "And I learned my healthy eating habits from you."

"No, Rachel, that's not true," Dave corrected her. "We both learned these habits from our parents."

"Have it your way."

"All of us FBI agents have eaten healthy for most of our lives, going back to our days in Homicide," Dale explained. "If this wasn't the case, we would never be fit enough to chase criminals."

"You have a point there," Melissa joked. "So many cops eat only doughnuts and coffee, especially in New York. Some of those men and women are so big and overweight they couldn't chase criminals to save their lives."

"Where I come from, up in Boston, Massachusetts," Tony said, "law enforcement have a saying: If you want criminals to get away with offenses and laugh at the law, eat as much food and drink as you want. Including coffee and doughnuts."

"Coffee is well cool," Dave remarked. "But when I had three doughnuts in a bakery, I threw up afterward. My healthy eating has adapted my metabolism to eating only healthy food, juices and water, not junk food."

"I think you'll cope with a Chinese dish and rice," Rachel promised him.

"Chinese is good," Tony agreed.

"Speaking of which," Dave said, "looks like our food is ready."

A man called out to them all in Chinese.

"Are those our dishes?" Tony called back.

The Chinese guy nodded his head.

"Thanks a lot," Dave said.

"Thanks for being patient." The Chinese man praised the FBI agents.

"How much are those dishes?" Dave asked.

"Fifty dollars in total."

They each passed over ten dollars.

"Thanks and a thousand thanks," Rachel called before all five vacated the Chinese restaurant. She turned toward the FBI agents. "We'll buy five bottles of fizzy drinks from that newspaper shop over there."

***

Back at Rachel's place, they dined with gusto on the five dishes and rice before consuming their drinks. They were heavily full of food and felt exhausted.

"Did you all enjoy your meals?" Rachel asked them.

"We did, sister." Dave chuckled.

"Without a doubt," Dale said.

"Was it the best Chinese you've ever had?" Melissa said, a smile beaming across her feminine face.

"Not the best," Dale said.

"I agree," she replied. "I've had better Chinese food in San Francisco and Timlook. But this food was just okay. Only just."

"You didn't enjoy it really," Dale objected.

"I did, but I've had better."

"What about you, Tony?" Rachel asked.

"It could've done with more salt and pepper," Tony complained. "But the spices were well cool. I mean, they were hot or medium spices, but the style was well cool."

"Cool being the word," Dave butted in. "Anyway, I'm tired. How about Tony sleeps in the first house, Dale and Melissa sleep in the second house, and I sleep in this place in the spare room?"

"Is that okay with all of you?" Tony asked.

"Yeah, definitely," they all confirmed.

"We'll sleep naked," Dave ordered. "Since we've already had showers, we'll put on the same clothes tomorrow morning as we've worn this afternoon. Then we'll buy food in Philadelphia."

Luis Calvera and Ramon Batista and the four other Cubans who had survived their jeep plunging into Lake Jacob had hired a Volvo and were now driving north to the outskirts of Lancaster County. Calvera scratched his moustache whilst Batista rubbed his beard, the other Cubans doing the same. All six mobsters felt their facial hair drenched with sweat as the sunshine beat down upon them through the Volvo's windows.

Calvera addressed the other guys. "Lancaster County is Amish country. But Bradley is a Quaker, and his family live around Lancaster County. We don't know the license plate of the vehicle those FBI agents were driving, but I can phone Timlook PD and impersonate Captain Robert Delarno at Lincoln PD. We'll get the cops at Timlook PD to run an APB on their vehicle and trace its location. Then we'll find FBI Agent Dave Bradley, the other three agents and Dave's sister. It will be a piece of cake."

Batista and the other Cubans laughed. Calvera dialed 911, and he got the operator.

"Hi there, this is the emergency center. Do you want the police, the fire service or the ambulance service?"

"It's Captain Robert Delarno of Lincoln PD, Pennsylvania," Calvera said. "I must call Captain Nicole Lamenski at Timlook PD, Pennsylvania, about a missing car."

"I'll put you through," the operator told him. There were a few bleeps, and then a woman's voice replied from Timlook PD.

"Hi there. Timlook PD, Captain Nicole Lamenski answering your call. Who is it?"

"It's Captain Robert Delarno of Lincoln PD," Calvera lied. "This concerns a missing vehicle belonging to Timlook PD, a car FBI Agent Dave Bradley was driving, accompanied by Agents Tony Selma, Dale Manuchi and Melissa Morgan. We are worried for the safety of these four FBI agents. Can you do an APB on this vehicle's license plate so we can pinpoint the vehicle's exact location? It's very important."

"I'll make my way to the computer room now. Just hang on a moment."

Nicole covered the distance from her office, through the main office, to the Computer Room. Already knowing the car's license plate, she ran an APB on the vehicle and then traced its exact location at that moment in time. Then she returned to her office.

"Hi, Captain Delarno, are you still there?" Nicole asked.

"I am still here."

"Dave Bradley's vehicle is at the Quaker hamlet of three farmhouses between Lancaster County and Philadelphia," she explained. "The Quaker hamlet is three miles west of Philadelphia's suburbs, in the countryside leading toward Lancaster County. Agents Bradley, Selma, Manuchi and Morgan are at Bradley's sister's place, which is one of the three farmhouses.

"Dave Bradley's sister is called Rachel Bradley, and she lives alone, but the four FBI agents are staying with her. Are Dave and the other agents okay?"

"They probably are, if they're with Dave's sister," Calvera said. "Thanks very much, Nicole. You've been a great help."

"It's my pleasure. Have a nice day."

"We will."

Calvera pressed his phone's power button. Then he turned toward Batista and the other mobsters. "There's a Quaker hamlet of three farmhouses, three miles from Philadelphia's outskirts. Dave Bradley's sister, Rachel, lives in one of these farmhouses. The APB on his vehicle's license plate traced the vehicle to this hamlet. This means the FBI agents are at the Quaker hamlet with Rachel Bradley. We must leave Lancaster County immediately."

Dave and Rachel had cereal for breakfast, and Tony, Dale and Melissa had eggs and sausages. Then Dave, Tony and Melissa made their way outside the house to admire the countryside. But Rachel took Dale by the arm before he could follow after them.

"What is it?" Dale asked.

"Some tomato sauce on your beard," Rachel said. "The tomato sauce you had with your eggs and sausages. I have a cloth here."

"Carry on," Dale invited her.

She wiped his mouth and the hairs around it until not a speck of sauce remained.

"The tomato sauce is gone. You know what, Dale?"

"What is it?" he said.

"You're so handsome, so good-looking." She chuckled. "Your wife Melissa is also pretty. I want to know what it's like to kiss a handsome man like you. How it feels."

She craned her neck and her lips met his. She caressed his shoulders underneath his white shirt and kissed him two more times. All three kisses told Dale that she had a serious crush on him.

Then Melissa was at the front door.

"Oh my God!" she exclaimed. "What are you doing?"

"Hey, wait, Melissa!" Dale cried. "It's not what you think!"

"Look, I'm sorry!" Rachel shouted. "It's my fault!"

Dale followed Melissa outside the door. Then he was in the farmyard but could not see her.

"Melissa, where are you?" he called.

"I'm here!" She came up behind him, and he turned to face her. "You bastard!" she yelled.

She swung her arm back and threw a fast karate punch into his nose with violent fury. His nostrils streamed blood, and he cried out at the burning pain, clutching his nose. The blood soaked his right hand.

"Ow, Melissa!" he screamed. "That really hurt! You didn't have to use your karate on me. I didn't know Rachel was going to kiss me—it was unexpected! I can explain!"

"You think I'm dumb, you asshole!" Melissa shouted. "But my karate and self-defense skills are not dumb!"

She threw a savage kick into his hips, and then three vicious punches into his stomach, before landing two more blows to his face.

Dale grabbed her wiry arms, but she lashed out at his face and chest with her elbows.

"Let me go," Melissa said.

"You must stop attacking me!" Dale cried. "I can explain!"

He seized her arms again and held her at arm's distance.

"It was my fault," Rachel said. "Dale didn't kiss me. I kissed him."

As Dale's strong hands gripped Melissa's narrow shoulders, she calmed down.

"Am I supposed to believe that?" she asked.

"It's true," Dale promised her. "Rachel came on to me."

Dave and Tony approached the three of them.

"Why were you beating up on your husband?" Dave shouted.

"You're supposed to love Dale, not beat him up," Tony growled.

"I made a mistake," Melissa whimpered. "I thought he had cheated on me. I'm sorry, Dale."

"Think nothing of it," Dale told her. "Just don't hit me again."

"I kissed Dale," Rachel told them again.

"You kissed Dale!" Dave exclaimed. "No wonder Melissa misunderstood what was happening! Don't do that again, Rachel!"

"I promise I won't," Rachel assured Dave.

"You make sure you don't," Melissa demanded. Her sharp eyes gave Rachel a hard, serious stare, and Dave's sister realized Dale's wife was not a woman to be taken for granted.

"She's got the message, Melissa," Dave reassured her.

"To change the subject…" Tony began.

"We must help you with a shopping trip to a chain store in Philadelphia," Dale told Rachel.

"Was that what you were about to say, Tony?" Melissa asked.

"Yes, it was."

"Before Dale rudely butted in," Dave said. "But I'll write a shopping list for Rachel, and then we'll set off for our big shopping spree to buy food."

"You need more food," Melissa told Rachel.

"We'll stop by at a cafe afterward," Dale suggested.

"A cafe, Dale?" Tony asked.

"We'll have a small lunch."

"Great idea," Melissa agreed.

"Are you up for that, Dave, Rachel?" Tony asked.

"It'll save me cooking," Rachel said.

"Then a cafe it will be," Dave said.

***

They loaded all the groceries into the two cars, and then Rachel drove herself and Dave in her own car toward Tandino's Cafe in Philadelphia's northern suburbs. Dale drove himself, Melissa and Tony in Timlook PD's civilian car.

"You know about Tandino's Cafe?" Rachel asked.

"I don't," Dave said. "Sounds like an Italian name."

"Benito Tandino and his family own the cafe," Rachel explained. "They came over to Philadelphia from Italy, and they make the best pizzas in Philadelphia. I know we're all into healthy eating, but do you fancy a pizza for lunch?"

"I reckon I can get away with a pizza," Dave boasted. "I've stayed slim for so many years that even a big pizza or mega-sized pizza won't make too much difference to my weight. I'll also have a bottle of root beer. How about you, sister?"

"I'll have a large pizza," Rachel said. "Do all four of you like pizza?"

"I reckon so," Dave told her. "How long have you known Benito Tandino?"

"Three years. And when I tell you Tandino's pizzas are the city's best pizzas, and even the best in all of Pennsylvania, you'd better believe it. He is the best, the great, the outstanding pizza chef, Mister Tandino."

"I believe it," Dave chuckled. "And we're at Tandino's Cafe now."

Rachel pulled the car to a halt and then turned her key inside the ignition, switching off the vehicle's engine. They pushed open the doors, climbed outside and then shut the doors before Rachel activated the locking mechanism. Tony, Dale and Melissa came toward them.

"I'll look forward to what Tandino's Cafe has to offer," Tony remarked.

"Rachel told us earlier they specialize in pizzas," Dale said. "The best pizzas in Pennsylvania."

"Do you both fancy pizzas?" Melissa asked. "I do."

"I fancy a pizza," Tony replied.

"Then we'll each have a pizza," Dale decided.

They entered Tandino's Cafe. A middle-aged man of fifty-three approached them with five menus.

"Hi there, it's me, the great pizza chef Benito Tandino! Do you all want drinks before your pizzas—or any other Italian dish of your choice?"

"Yeah, we will," Dave agreed. "I'll have a root beer."

"I'll have an American ginger beer," Melissa ordered.

"I'll have a Coke on the rocks," Dale told Tandino.

"A lemonade on the rocks," Tony added.

"A Tango Orange for me," said Rachel.

"Do you want to look at the menu?" Tandino asked.

"We've all decided to eat your pizzas," Rachel told him. "The best pizzas in Pennsylvania."

"Even better than the Pizza Land or Pizza Hut joints," Melissa told everybody.

"Or Domino's," Dale remarked.

"I'll have a chicken tandoori pizza," Tony decided.

"A giant mega-sized pizza for me," Dave asked. "And it will be a meat feast."

"A vegetarian pizza," Dale told him.

"And the same for me," Melissa ordered. "A vegetarian pizza."

"A chicken and mushroom pizza for me," Rachel enthused.

"Okay, ladies and gentlemen," Tandino announced, "your pizzas will be ready in half an hour's time. Your drinks are coming up now. Do you want baskets of bread to whet your appetites? Well-baked Italian bread, of course."

"Why not?" Tony said. "We'll have two baskets of bread."

"Don't you think you're overdoing it, Tony?" Dale objected. "Us cops are on a limited budget, and we've already paid twenty dollars each for groceries."

"No, he's not overdoing it, my love," Melissa told him.

"Today is Wednesday," Dave explained. "We'll get paid on Friday. By my wife, Captain Nicole Lamenski."

"At the end of this week," Tony said.

"In that case, we'll have two baskets of bread," Dave told the chef.

"I like your style, Dave," Rachel said.

"Drinks and bread coming right up," Tandino confirmed.

***

At Timlook PD, Nicole was in her office eating KFC with French fries, onion rings and a huge cardboard cup of lemonade for lunch. As soon as she had finished consuming her meal and drink, the office phone rang. She answered it.

"Hi there. Timlook Police Department, Captain Nicole Lamenski taking your call. Who is it?"

"It's Captain Robert Delarno of Lincoln PD. We've made a grisly discovery at Lake Jacob thirty miles from Lancaster County. We found three burned-out trucks on the side road and an upside-down jeep in the lake. The two Cubans in the jeep's front seats were shot to death, and their bodies were strapped upside-down in their seats underwater. The mutilated corpses of thirty

Cubans were found in and around the three trucks, badly burned. Trails of gasoline led behind the trucks, and it's likely FBI Agent Dave Bradley and his team fired into these trails, igniting the fuel, which burned toward the trucks' fuel tanks. We found bullets at the beginning of these trails in the road. The three explosions that followed killed all thirty Cubans, wiping out the whole of Luis Calvera's mob. But there was no sign of Timlook PD's car or of Agents Dave Bradley, Tony Selma, Dale Manuchi or Melissa Morgan.

"By the tire tracks in the road, their car was driven away, which means they survived this confrontation with Luis Calvera, Ramon Batista and their mobsters."

"They survived!" Nicole exclaimed. "Thank God! Is that why you phoned me earlier to ask for the APB on Timlook PD's car? So you could find out if Dave's people were okay? I told you the vehicle was traced to Rachel Bradley's place, the Quaker hamlet outside Lancaster County?"

"I never phoned you earlier," Delarno said. "And I never inquired about any missing vehicle or whether or not Dave's people were okay. This whole morning, due to a tip-off from a young couple hiking near Lake Jacob, a team of cops and I, together with Forensics and CSI people, were driving toward Lake Jacob to examine the scene of the massacre. Maybe the man who phoned you this morning was a crank caller?"

"Oh my God!" Nicole cried. "He wasn't a crank caller. It was more dangerous than that. I must ask you a question."

"What?"

"Did you find Calvera and Batista's bodies in the trucks, or the jeep which crashed into the lake?"

"There was no sign of Calvera or Batista," Delarno told Nicole. "In the mud and the embankment overlooking the lake, we found six sets of shoeprints. Which means six Cubans escaped from the jeep in the lake, and two of them were Calvera and Batista."

"Okay, thank you," Nicole snapped. "I must make a call to Dave."

Nicole and Delarno ended the telephone call. From her jacket pocket, she pulled out her cellphone and dialed Dave's number. "Answer me, Dave," she pleaded.

***

Rachel, Dave and the other FBI agents were chewing down their pizzas, and Dave turned to the others. "Are you all enjoying your pizzas?"

Rachel was the first to reply. "I am," she enthused. "These pizzas really are the best."

"I agree with that entirely," Tony remarked.

"I couldn't fault my pizza for the world," Dale said.

"This is brilliant," Melissa agreed. "But I still prefer the pizzas from Domino's or Papa John's."

"This was great pizza," Dave added.

"Great pizza, Dave?" Tony asked. "But not the best."

"I've had better pizza at Pizza Hut," Dave pointed out.

"Never mind," Rachel snapped. "I can't say I didn't try."

"Oh, it was great," Dave explained. "And I would come to Tandino's Cafe again. I can't fault these pizzas for the whole of America." Then he heard his cellphone bleeping. "That's my phone; I must answer it." As he stood up from his chair, he produced the cellphone from his jeans pocket. "Hi there, FBI Agent Dave Bradley here. Who's calling?"

"It's your wife, Nicole, calling from Timlook PD. Are the four of you and Rachel okay, after you survived that confrontation with Calvera and Batista's mob at Lake Jacob?"

"We're okay," Dave promised her. "We killed Calvera, Batista and all their mobsters at the lake. Six mobsters, including the two arms dealers, drowned when their jeep crashed into the lake. We're having lunch at Tandino's Cafe in Philadelphia, after buying food in Philadelphia's main chain store. But how do you know about that confrontation at Lake Jacob? I never called you to tell you we were okay."

"Captain Delarno called me from Lincoln PD and told me," Nicole explained. "I had another call an hour before from a man impersonating Delarno. He asked me to trace the exact location of your car, and the computer pinpointed it to your sister Rachel's place outside Lancaster County. And I told him you were at this place. For a Cuban, he faked an Italian American accent very well when he impersonated Delarno. This man was Calvera."

"You're kidding, right?" Dave snapped. "After Melissa shot two men in the eight-seater jeep's front seats, the jeep flew into the lake and the other men drowned. Including Calvera and Batista."

"Delarno told me these six men were never found," Nicole said, worried. "Which means they're alive and you're in danger."

"Thanks for the not-so-pleasant news," Dave told her.

"Be careful, Dave," Nicole warned him. "I have to go now. Good day."

"Good day."

They broke off contact, and he turned to Tony, Dale and Melissa. "Six Cubans, including Calvera and Batista, are still alive. They didn't drown when that jeep crashed into the lake."

"What do we do?" Dale asked.

"Be on our guard," Tony said.

"And have our weapons ready," Dale added.

"I'm scared, Dave," Rachel stammered. "And I mean terrified."

"We all are," Dave said.

"But we'll protect you," Tony reassured her.

"Just let us do our jobs," Melissa ordered.

"Any of you want another drink?" Tony asked. They all shook their heads.

"Nobody wants a drink," Dave pointed out. "We'd better pay the bill and then return to the Quaker hamlet."

After leaving Philadelphia, Dave and Rachel drove the two cars in the direction of Lancaster County. Then they turned both vehicles down the side road leading toward the Quaker hamlet.

Inside Rachel's car, Tony turned toward Dave's sister.

"I don't see any sign of the six Cubans or their vehicle," he told her.

"Does that mean we can relax?" Rachel asked.

"No, it doesn't. We'll check to see any sign of their car."

In Timlook PD's car, Dave turned to Dale and Melissa.

"I see no sign of Calvera's car or the six Cubans."

"We must still exercise caution at all times," Dale growled.

"How many rounds are there in the three rifles and the handgun?" Melissa asked. "Probably not enough."

"The rifles and the handgun are in the back seat, buried under the shopping bags," Dave told her. "We'll gather them fast and throw one rifle to Tony before we do a thorough search of the hamlet."

"There are tire tracks behind the cattle barn," Dale said. "Those tracks weren't there when we left the hamlet."

"Everybody, duck now!" Dave cried.

They just managed to before the bulletproof windshield and windows were cracked by rifle shots, only one second later.

"Get out of the car!"

Pushing open the doors, they rolled outside the vehicle, and Tony joined them. Rachel was behind him, and Dave saw that the windshield and windows of Rachel's car were shattered to smithereens. Her car did not have bulletproof windows.

"Oh my God!" Rachel stammered.

"Don't panic!" Tony ordered.

"No, don't, Rachel," Dave repeated.

"I'm going inside what was the Petersons' house." Rachel sobbed.

"No, you stay with us," Dave whispered.

"I'm scared," she whimpered. "I'll open the door so we all escape."

She leaped to her feet and ran for the front door.

"No wait, Rachel!" Dave yelled. But a savage gunshot echoed through the air before a large bullet penetrated her shoulder. Rachel screamed with vicious agony before she flew forward, hit her head on the front door and blacked out on the porch.

"Jesus Christ!" Dave shouted.

"We must get the rifles and the handgun," Dale whispered.

"No, the guns are out of our reach," Melissa warned him. "Buried under the groceries. They'll shoot us before we even lay a hand on our weapons."

"She's right, Dale," Dave agreed. "We must head round the back of the other two houses and draw the Cubans away from Rachel. She's not dead. I hear her breathing."

"Will that work?" Tony asked.

"It had better work," Dave said. "We must use our martial arts skills against these arms dealers. Hand-to-hand fighting is no match against high-caliber rifles, so we must take them by surprise. The element of surprise is a formidable advantage in combat when you don't have a gun."

"We'd better chance it," Tony said.

"Calvera, Batista!" Dave shouted. "We're making our way behind the two houses!"

"We have no weapons!" Tony called. "So try to catch us if you can!"

"Come and get us, you assholes!" Dave cried. He addressed the other three. "When I say run, you run. Are you ready?"

Dale and Melissa nodded their heads.

"We're ready," Tony whispered.

"Run for it now—and I mean now!"

All four FBI agents leaped to their feet and sprinted around the corner of the second Quaker house, then made their way behind both Quaker houses. A vicious hail of gunshots punched large holes into the woodwork and shattered the windows, but the FBI agents escaped just in time. Then Calvera, Batista and the other four Cubans raced toward the two houses.

"You two, go round the south side of the far house whilst you go between the two houses!" Calvera cried. "The fourth guy, Batista and I will run along the north side of the nearest house! We'll trap the FBI agents between our three attacks by encircling them!"

"What do we do about Rachel?" Batista asked.

"She's dead," Calvera said. "We leave her where she is. And concentrate on encircling and outnumbering the four FBI agents. Six of us against four of them."

"Six against four." A Cuban chuckled. "Not bad odds."

"Let's go, guys!" Calvera shouted.

On the far house's south side, the two Cubans were cautious.

They turned the corner onto the west side, but even with their powerful rifles, they were no match for a surprise attack. And it came so fast and so hard they did not know what hit them. Using the metal lids from two garbage cans, Dale and Tony bashed the Cubans' arms, knocking the rifles out of their hands. Dale and the first Cuban charged into each other, but the Cuban was much larger and stronger than Dale. He grabbed Dale's throat, but Dale used the momentum of his attack to fall backward in a somersault with his foot embedded into the guy's stomach and hurled the guy through the air. The mobster landed flat on his back but was immune to pain and scrambled off the ground again. Dale was up off the ground, charged the guy and smashed his fist square into the brute's jaw. This fearsome blow split open the Cuban's jaw before two more blows knocked his bottom teeth out. With a broken jaw and broken teeth, the Cuban's mouth spurted blood, but he hurled two blows toward Dale's eyes. Dale's eyes were blackened with bruises before he grabbed the guy's arm, twisted it around behind his back and wrenched it with force. With a crack, the arm broke. One last punch to the Cuban's throat broke his windpipe before the man gasped and hurtled to the ground, clutching his throat. He died soon after.

While Dale fought the first Cuban, Tony charged into the second and bashed the man's elbow against the wall, making the hardened criminal release his grip on the rifle. The Cuban punched Tony in the stomach followed by two blows to his mouth, but then Tony landed a fearsome punch to the man's groin. Screaming in excruciating pain, he doubled up before Tony smashed three punches into the criminal's mouth. The brute's broken jaw distorted his face and sent blood gushing into the air, but he still fought with all his strength.

They exchanged punches to each other's faces, but Dale grabbed the first guy's rifle, rammed it against the second man's throat from behind and, with a violent twist of the enormous weapon, snapped the guy's neck.

"Thanks, Dale," Tony said. "I owe you one."

"Think nothing of it," Dale said.

***

Between the two houses, the third Cuban was taken by surprise by Melissa. She bashed the metal lid of a trash can into his face, but he tightened his grip on the rifle. Melissa threw three fast punches into his nose and mouth, then two blows to his stomach and solar plexus before landing a vicious kick into his hips. The guy fell over, and Melissa grabbed the garbage can's lid again. The man scrambled off the ground and bashed at Melissa with his rifle, but Melissa shielded her head and body with the lid. She whacked him in the face with the lid, and then their weapons collided.

With one violent clang of the lid, the brute's rifle flew from his hands, but he produced from his leather jacket a large flick knife, which shot open. The man kicked the metal lid out of Melissa's hands before he lunged with the knife. Melissa grabbed his wrists, and there was a grappling match between the two of them. He was much stronger than Melissa, and the knife came down toward her throat. But in the last second, Melissa dodged aside and deflected the guy's hands downward so the knife plunged into his stomach. She pulled the knife out and then thrust the blade into the man's solar plexus. He staggered back, the knife stuck inside his sternum. Blood ran from his mouth as his eyes widened, and then he dropped into a heap on the ground.

"You weren't expecting that, you bastard!" Melissa cried.

***

Calvera, Batista and the fourth Cuban moved from the north side of the closest house to the west side, where they were unprepared for Dave's violent attack. With a savage kick, his foot ploughed viciously into Calvera's groin, flooring him for a minute.

Lunging with his car keys, which cut like a knife, he slashed the fourth Cuban's face and gouged his eye. The Cuban screamed with agony, clutching his face, before Batista threw three blows into Dave's face. His mouth and nose were bleeding, but then he rammed two punches into Batista's stomach and solar plexus and three blows to his face. The first punch splattered Batista's nose and sent blood gushing down his face. The other two blows blackened his eyes before Dave sent a kick flying into the guy's groin. Batista screamed with appalling agony, and then Dave pressed home his vicious attack. A punch to the stomach ruptured the brute's insides, and then Dave smashed two more punches, which smeared Batista's nose all over his face, blood soaking his beard. With a hand strike, Dave forced the bridge of his nose through his head and into his brain, killing him instantly.

The fourth Cuban came at Dave, but Dave elbowed him in the stomach, threw him aside and then punched him in the throat. The guy's windpipe snapped and the brute grabbed his throat, fell to the ground and died in four or five seconds.

But Dave's kick to Calvera's groin had only floored him for a minute. He charged up from the ground and punched Dave in the head. Dave seized his arm, threw him toward the wall, and then grabbed Calvera's rifle off the ground. Calvera charged, and they grappled over the rifle, the barrel dangerously close to Dave's head. Dave kneed him in the groin, then head-butted him in the eye, and the mobster screamed with terrifying pain. He hurtled backward before two sideways kicks from Dave's foot snapped Calvera's thigh bone above his knee. Calvera screamed again, dropping to the ground. Dave turned the rifle sharply toward him.

"Go ahead and kill me!" Calvera growled.

"I've never gotten used to killing people," Dave said. "But I won't lose sleep over ridding the world of scum like you."

Squeezing the trigger, he pumped three deafening gunshots into Calvera's chest, the bullets ripping apart his heart and lungs and smearing his body with blood. More blood trickled from his mouth as he died.

Dave dropped the rifle. Melissa ran up to him.

"Are you okay, Dave?" she cried.

"Yes, I am," Dave said. "Calvera, Batista and their arms trafficking ring will never bother us again."

"That was great fighting. You should've seen me take on the third Cuban and come out on top."

"Whilst we took on the first two guys," Tony added.

"We've forgotten something," Dale realized. "Is Rachel okay?"

"I must check on Rachel," Dave said. "One of you, call an ambulance."

"Can you forgive me, Melissa?" Dale asked. "For the way Rachel kissed me."

"All is forgiven and forgotten." Melissa chuckled, and she kissed him on the mouth.

Tony reached for his cellphone and dialed 911 for the ambulance service and the Philadelphia police. Dave darted around the house to the porch. He crouched beside Rachel as she lay on the porch knocked out cold. He checked her breathing and her pulse. She was breathing faintly, and her pulse was still beating.

"Rachel, can you hear me?" Dave said. "Tony has called the police and the ambulance. We're taking you to hospital."

"She'll be okay, won't she?" Dale asked.

"Don't worry, honey." Melissa comforted him. "She will."

"They'll be here in ten minutes," Tony promised Dave.

"All we can do is wait," Dave said.

***

At Philadelphia Hospital, Dave made a call to Nicole. She answered after three bleeps.

"Hi there, Captain Nicole Lamenski replying to your call. Is that you, Dave?"

"It is me. The nightmare is over. Calvera and Batista and their arms dealers are dead. Us four FBI agents took down the mobsters at the Quaker hamlet. Rachel was shot but is now stable. The cops will question us. How are you?"

"I was worried about you," Nicole said. "But I'm glad the four of you are okay. Wish Rachel the best from me."

"I will," Dave said. "I have to go now. Goodbye, Nicole."

"Goodbye, honey." Nicole chuckled. "I'll pay all of you your salaries tomorrow, Friday."

***

In a hospital bed, Rachel regained consciousness and opened her eyes. Melissa leaned over and kissed Rachel's mouth, their brows touching. Then Melissa withdrew and smiled brightly as her hand swiped a few hairs away from her forehead. She sat down in a chair between Dale and Tony.

"How are you, Rachel?" Dale asked.

"You've recovered remarkably," Melissa said.

"Dave will come soon," Tony told her.

"I'm still badly shaken by the shooting," Rachel said. "But I'm okay."

"Dave is phoning Nicole," Tony continued, "and he's finished his call. He's coming now."

"Dave!" Rachel exclaimed. "Thank you for coming."

"It's my pleasure, little sister," Dave chuckled.

A nurse came over.

"When will Rachel be discharged?" he asked her.

"Tomorrow morning at ten."

NO GREATER WICKEDNESS

In South Timlook's Athens Street, FBI Agents Dave Bradley and Tony Selma were buying some Greek food at a taverna. Dave bought a kebab with rice whilst Tony purchased a plate full of kofta and rice. They had almost finished their meals.

"You enjoyed your meal?" Dave asked.

"You bet I did, Dave," Tony said. "You bet."

"Fancy some ouzo?"

"No, but do you? You're driving, remember."

"Good thinking," Dave agreed. "I'll pass on that."

Then three Cuban men stormed into the taverna through the front entrance, brandishing rifles. One was moustached, the other two bearded.

"Okay, down on the floor, all of you!" the moustached guy cried. His yelling was extremely violent, and men, women and children screamed and cried with petrified terror and horror. "Hand over your money now! All of you!"

Dave and Tony reached inside their FBI uniforms for their handguns, focused the weapons on the three men and opened fire. Two shots from Dave's piece felled the man with the moustache before three more blasts dropped one of the bearded guys. Tony blazed three gunshots into the third criminal. Their chests smeared crimson with blood, the brutes hurtled to the floor and died instantly.

"It's okay now!" Dave shouted to the cowering people.

"You can relax!" Tony added.

The men, women and children were badly shaken by this dangerous ordeal but were also staring at Dave and Tony with gratitude for saving them. Dave turned toward the taverna's manager.

"You mind calling Timlook PD?" he asked. "We're FBI Agents Dave Bradley and Tony Selma. Dial 911. When the operator passes you over to Timlook PD, tell them we've shot and killed three criminals who were about to rob customers at gunpoint. We want the Forensics and CSI people over here fast."

"I got it," the manager replied.

The uniforms, Forensics and CSI were at the scene in ten minutes. Captain Nicole

Lamenski was with the uniformed police, and she approached Dave and Tony.

"Run me through what happened," she said.

"Well, Nicole," Dave told her, "these three guys thought they would have an easy ride raiding this Greek taverna and robbing all the customers. They didn't see Agent Selma and myself sitting at our table, having finished our meals. We drew our handguns and fired before they could shoot back at us. There were three of them against two of us, so we didn't take any chances with our own safety or the customers'."

"It was them or us," Tony added.

"It seems that way, yes," Dave pointed out. "These guys were Cubans, and their rifles were AK-47s."

"You have a point there," Nicole said. "What are you telling me? That arms dealers are involved?"

"It's December 29th, 2021 now," Tony said. "In three days' time, it will be 2022."

"Your point being?"

"The three of us haven't celebrated Christmas," Tony finished off. "If we're suspended, can we have our Christmas break?"

"Sure you can."

"But first things first," Tony said.

"Carry on, Tony."

"We'll have a ballistics report done on the AK-47s and their bullets," Dave butted in. "Then use the rifles' serial numbers to trace the weapons back to the arms dealer who supplied those weapons. Then we'll hunt him down, like we did Luis Calvera and Ramon Batista nearly two years ago, early in 2020. Calvera has a son named Alonso Calvera who was released from Philadelphia Prison in November 2021 for running a street gang. He is also into arms dealing and maybe sent those three Cubans to kill us. Otherwise, why would they pick this Greek taverna, of all places?"

"They were robbing customers," Tony said.

"But with AK-47 assault rifles?" Dave asked. "Shortly after Alonso was released, two attempts were made on our lives in Madrid Street and Milan Street, again by Cubans with AK-47 assault rifles. Robbing the customers was just a cover for something much bigger."

"Like popping both of you," Nicole said. "And you think Alonso was behind the attempted hits?"

"I do," Dave told her. "In the first two hits, the Cubans got away with their weapons, so we couldn't trace the serial numbers, but now these three guys are dead, we can run a check on the rifles' serial numbers and trace them back to the arms dealer who supplied them."

"After you've done that," Nicole said, "I won't suspend you without pay, but I'll give you a week off work. Paid vacation, of course."

"You know what?" Tony said.

"We could all do with a break," Dave finished.

***

The ballistics report took ten minutes. After that was done, the rifles' serial numbers were traced to a young Cuban arms dealer with a Mexican-style moustache standing five feet eight inches tall.

"The three Cubans were working for this young man, Alonso Calvera, son of Luis Calvera," Dave began. "He is twenty-three years old and started his criminal record at sixteen when his street gang massacred a rival street gang in Philadelphia. Tried as a juvenile who was corrupted by his father, he got a lenient sentence of ten years, which was reduced to seven when he was released in November 2021."

"That's not all," Tony remarked. "Three attempts were made on our lives in Madrid, Milan and Athens Streets, all by Cubans with AK-47 assault rifles. We failed to nail the Cubans in Madrid Street and Milan Street, but we got them in Athens Street, at that Greek taverna. We'll begin 2022 hunting for Alonso Calvera."

"But first, take a week off," Nicole ordered.

***

Dave and Tony were in Lomax's Saloon on Turin Street, and due to taking a vacation off work, they were each drinking an American ginger beer. They were joined by the former leader of Timlook Vice Squad, Richard Kanaris. Even in his mid-sixties and now retired, Kanaris had long brown hair turning grey and a thick beard. He had commanded a squad of three bearded cops named Jan Muller, John Felt and Matt Felder, and a blond-haired cop with a moustache and glasses, Mark Blondel. These guys were now leading SWAT teams all over Pennsylvania and Maryland, but Kanaris himself had retired three years ago.

"Well, look who we have here!" Dave cried.

"You know him?" Tony asked.

"Sure I do."

"Long time, no see," Kanaris chuckled. "How you doing?"

"Pretty cool." Dave laughed.

"More like well cool," Tony said. "What's your name?"

"Richard Kanaris. I used to run Timlook Vice Squad, five of us hippy cops pulling undercover operations throughout this city. Now I'm retired. What's your name?"

"Tony Selma. FBI Agent Tony Selma. I'm from Boston, Massachusetts. I'm the new partner of FBI Agent Dave Bradley. You know each other?"

"We go back a long way, Agent Selma."

"Call me Tony."

"And call me Dave, not Agent Bradley," Dave asked Kanaris.

"Okay, Dave and Tony," Kanaris began. "It's good to see young blood like you in the force. How are you finding the FBI?"

"It has its moments," Tony told him. "They say young people are our future."

"Too right," Kanaris agreed. He turned to Dave. "So, you're an FBI agent now? After all those years you worked in Homicide. You and I go back nearly twenty-two years, to the Jingles and Mck-Fee drug cartel case in 2000. Then the Donald Helsing case in 2007, and the second Mck-Fee Cartel case in 2009, where we all smashed the New England Net, a network of drug cartels throughout the northeastern United States, after Matt and Ray Mck-Fee and their mob pursued you from Chicago to Timlook. My vice squad are now leading SWAT teams in Virginia, Maryland and Pennsylvania, whilst John Reynolds and Bernardo Ruiz are retired. Nicole Lamenski is now Captain of Timlook PD.

"But two years ago, I heard the tragic news of James Mitchell's death in that shootout at the National Pennsylvania Bank. Of all people, Jim was the last man in the world who deserved that."

"It was tragic," Dave told him.

"Too right it was," Kanaris said.

"But the good news is—" Tony began. Then Dave butted in.

"We massacred the arms dealers responsible. On Rachel Bradley's Quaker farmstead. These six guys included the top dealers Luis Calvera and Ramon Batista. But Calvera left a son, a two-faced punk named Alonso Calvera, who was recently released from Philadelphia Prison. He had served seven years for leading a street gang of hooligans in massacring a rival street gang. Since his release in November, he has upgraded his career from leading a street gang to arms dealing. In three hit operations, three gangs of Cubans on his payroll tried to pump lead into us.

"On the third occasion in Athens Street, we killed three of them and traced their weapons to Alonso Calvera. Following in his father's footsteps, he leads an arms trafficking ring and a violent street gang in Philadelphia."

"He is bad news," Tony said.

"I'll bet," Kanaris agreed. "Are Dale Manuchi and Melissa Morgan still working in Homicide?"

"They too are FBI agents like me and Tony," Dave explained. "And we're due to drop in on them at the Barracuda Restaurant overlooking the river, where they're having lunch."

"We're sorry to cut our conversation short," Tony said.

"Don't worry." Kanaris chuckled. "Have a nice day."

"We will," Dave said. "And the same to you."

"Have a nice day, Detective Kanaris," Tony said.

***

After stopping Timlook PD's civilian car outside the Barracuda Restaurant, Dave and Tony vacated the vehicle and ambled toward Dale and Melissa's table overlooking the river.

"There's lots of delicious food here," Dale said. "Including fish dishes."

"Hey, Dale!" Melissa said enthusiastically. "Dave and Tony are dropping in on us!" She laughed, and then her beaming smile turned into a sharp grin. Her hand swiped her long, dark hair away from her bare forehead.

"Hi there," Dave said.

"Can we eat with them?" Tony asked him.

"No, we're eating sandwiches," Dave replied. "We must watch our money."

"Are you kidding?" Melissa chuckled. "Come on, Dave. Don't be so mean."

"No, don't," Dale asserted.

"Dave is right," Tony said. "We must watch our money. But you two have fun."

"Get yourself a drink," Dave ordered. "It's on me."

"Thanks, and a thousand thanks," Tony replied.

Dave passed him two dollars to buy himself a Coke or lemonade. Then Dale and Melissa spotted five bearded Cubans walking with aggressive, menacing strides behind Dave and Tony and reaching for automatic revolvers inside their leather jackets.

"Quick! Dave, Tony, get down!" Melissa exclaimed.

She and Dale sprang up from their seats, dived into Dave and Tony, and all four agents plummeted to the ground. The Cubans opened fire but missed. Dave, Tony, Dale and Melissa produced handguns from their leather jackets and returned fire. Three shots from Dale's weapon brought down the first two Cubans whilst two shots from Melissa's handgun felled the third. Dave and Tony each blazed five shots into the chests of the last two brutes, who died instantly.

"Oh my God!" Dale screamed.

"Are you two okay?" Melissa cried.

"I'm okay," Dave stammered.

"I am too," Tony said.

"Luckily there were no other customers here," Dave said. "We'll check on these guys who tried to pop us."

Dave and Tony trained their handguns on the dead Cubans to make sure they were no longer dangerous.

"They look very dead to me," Dale remarked.

"They were only carrying automatic revolvers," Melissa said.

"Why revolvers?" Tony asked. "They would've been more lethal carrying AK-47s, like those three guys who tried to kill us at that Greek taverna."

"AK-47s or other rifles could not be easily concealed inside their jackets," Dave explained. "If we spotted them coming toward us armed with AK-47 assault rifles, they would lose the element of surprise. That's why they carried automatic revolvers."

"Although not as lethal as the men who attacked you at the Greek tavern…" Dale began.

"They were deadly enough," Melissa finished.

"This is the fourth attempt on our lives," Dave growled. "Alonso Calvera is as dangerous as his father and is trying to avenge what we did to his father. I'll call the uniforms over here."

***

At Timlook PD, Nicole summoned the four FBI agents into her office.

"This is the fourth time Cubans have tried to kill you," she began. "And again, the serial numbers on the Cubans' revolvers can be traced back to Alonso Calvera. Do you think Alonso is bent on revenge for the killings of his father and his gang at Rachel's Quaker farmstead?"

"We don't think it," Dave said.

"We know it," Tony said.

"And there will be more attempts." Dale sounded worried.

"And they'll not only target Agents Bradley and Selma but they'll also target Agent Manuchi and me," Melissa told Nicole.

"If Alonso has a personal vendetta against my husband, then chances are there's a target on my back," Nicole said. "Which means the four of you and I must take a trip to Philadelphia and find him."

"You don't have to come to Philly with us," Dave offered her. "You can spend the next few weeks at Dale and Melissa's farmstead ten miles from Timlook, with over a dozen police officers protecting you. And for extra protection, you could carry your handgun, a rifle and three pepper sprays. The farmstead has been used before, to protect that Amish family, the von Hesses, during the Donald Helsing case back in 2007. But you can ask Dale and Melissa if it's okay by them."

"If we're away in Philadelphia," Melissa said, "Nicole and these police officers can have the farmstead all to themselves."

"What's your objection to me coming with you?" Nicole asked.

"No objection," Dave told her. "Only being higher up in the ranks, you're needed to hold the fort here in Timlook and command your teams to keep this city safe. With you joining us on the East Coast, who else is going to run this department from Melissa's farmstead? Finding a replacement is not always as easy as people think."

"You have a point," Nicole agreed. "In that case, the farmstead."

"In the meantime, your FBI chief, Mark Cavitis, wants you in his office at the FBI Headquarters. He was away on vacation, but he's come back. You need to see him."

***

At the FBI Headquarters on Warsaw Street in northeast Timlook, all four agents waited in the main office. Then a tall, muscled black man in a grey suit summoned them into the chief's office. He was Chief Mark Cavitis.

"Okay, Agents Bradley, Selma, Manuchi and Morgan!" he called. "In my office now!"

They got up from their chairs and made their way into Chief Cavitis's office.

"I heard about the four attempts to kill Bradley and Selma!" Cavitis bellowed. "And Alonso Calvera is behind it!"

"So why are you mad at us?" Dave asked.

"In the Greek taverna!" Cavitis roared. "You endangered the lives of innocent bystanders by shooting at the three Cubans! Then at the Barracuda Restaurant, you four endangered other customers by firing at the five Cubans who were about to shoot you! Why didn't you call for backup?"

"We didn't have time to call for backup," Tony said. "We had to react at the spur of the moment. In the Greek taverna, customers were out of our line of fire."

"Not only that," Dave told Cavitis, "but at the Barracuda Restaurant, few customers had come in, and they were on the restaurant's other side, overlooking the river."

"And no sooner did Melissa and I spot the five Cubans coming toward the table, than we both dived into Dave and Tony so we would all be out of the Cubans' line of fire," Dale said. "Had we not drawn our guns and killed these mobsters, these guys would've put all of us six feet underground."

"You would be attending our funerals," Melissa remarked.

"But we're all determined to find Alonso and his mob and bring them to justice," Tony said.

"So if you want Nicole to suspend us without pay for a week, we could use that time to head for Philadelphia and find Alonso," Dave suggested.

"You'll be suspended, but you'll still be paid," Cavitis told them. He was much calmer now. "In that case, set off for Philadelphia and find that bastard. You need backup?"

"We'll call Philadelphia PD if we need backup," Dave promised Cavitis. "But for the next few days, we must operate in that city without Alonso and his guys hatching on to our presence."

"Good luck," Cavitis said. "You'll need it."

***

With the FBI agents traveling in the car behind, Nicole drove her own car south toward Melissa's farmstead. Then they all left the vehicles, and Melissa turned her key in the house's front door.

Nicole turned toward Dave and Tony.

"When will the squad cars arrive with uniformed cops?" she asked Dave.

"They'll be here soon," he replied.

"I see them coming now," Tony said.

"Here's three pepper sprays for you, and my automatic revolver in case your handgun runs out of bullets," Melissa told Nicole.

"Dale and I have two rifles on our dining room wall for extra protection, but the guys in uniforms are here now, so you won't need those."

"The door's open, so make your way in," Dale said.

Nicole and Melissa entered, followed by Dave and Tony, and lastly Dale.

Tony and Nicole sat in armchairs while Dale and Melissa took the settee and Dave got up and approached the front door.

"You want to welcome the uniforms?" Nicole asked.

"I will," he said. "We'll spend the night here."

"And then make that trip to Philadelphia," Nicole agreed. "I still wish I could go with you. Instead, I'm stuck here surrounded by men and women in uniforms."

"You'll get used to it," Dave promised her.

"Sure I will."

Dave made his way outside.

"Hi there," he greeted the uniformed men and women.

"Hi there," they called back.

"The same to you, your FBI agents and to Captain Nicole Lamenski!" the sergeant roared.

"Your name, Sergeant?" Dave asked.

"Sergeant Rulio Diablo!" the moustached Cuban growled.

Turning his rifle on Dave, he aimed, but Dave was quicker to the draw. Rulio opened fire, but Dave dodged aside in the nick of time, focused his handgun on Rulio and fired two shots. Two bearded Cubans aimed their rifles, but the other cops jumped them to the ground.

Tony, Dale, Melissa and Nicole raced outside the farmhouse, also aiming their handguns.

Dave pointed his gun at the wounded Rulio. "Who sent you to kill me?"

"Alonso Calvera," Rulio groaned, pained.

"I see," Dave said. "Where's Alonso's hideout?"

"Tell us, fast!" Tony snapped. "We ain't got all day!"

"22 Madrid Street, Timlook's Spanish area," Rulio stammered.

Dave turned to the other two Cubans being pinned down by the uniformed cops.

"Is he telling the truth? 22 Madrid Street?"

"Si, Senor Bradley!" they shouted.

"Not far from where one of the first two attempts were made on our lives!" Tony realized. "Before the other two in Athens Street and the Barracuda Restaurant."

"We'd better make our way there now," Dave ordered. "And call other FBI agents to back us up. Nicole, Dale and Melissa must stay here with the uniforms."

"You're kidding, right?" Dale objected.

"No, he's not," Melissa said.

"Dave, honey," Nicole said. "Please be careful."

"I will," Dave promised her. "Tony, come with me."

"I'm on it."

***

The car screeched to a halt around the corner from 22 Madrid Street, and Dave and Tony reached for their handguns.

"The Feds are not here," Tony complained.

"We can do this without them," Dave growled.

They opened the vehicle's front doors and hurried outside, then sneaked their way toward the front door.

"Timlook Police, open up!" Dave shouted.

"Or we'll bash the door open!" Tony yelled.

"Are you ready?" Dave asked him.

Throwing their full weight against the door, they forced it off its hinges and raced inside. The dining room was full of automatic weapons.

Three Cubans trying to get rid of these weapons turned their rifles upon Dave and Tony, but the FBI agents blazed savagely. Dave shot one guy in the head, then another with two slugs to the chest. Tony fired two rounds into the third guy's chest, and all three mobsters hurtled to the carpet. Two other Cubans charged from the kitchen across the hallway and aimed their submachine guns, but the agents were ready for them. Dave and Tony each fired a gunshot to a man's head, and both guys crashed against the hallway's wall and slumped to the floor.

"We can't interrogate them now," Tony told Dave.

"No," Dave said. "But I see photos stuck to the wall in the bedroom ahead. Let's check it out."

They entered the bedroom and saw that the photos were of the people Alonso Calvera was targeting.

"This is like real psycho stuff," Dave remarked. "Like the MO of a serial killer taking photos of his victims."

"Alonso Calvera is a serial killer now?" Tony asked.

"Not quite. Most serial killers select victims at random and don't tend to target key individuals. Alonso is not enough of a psycho to do that. All his intended targets are people he holds responsible for the deaths of his father, Luis Calvera, and Ramon Batista and their arms trafficking ring. There are three photos of me and two of you. There are three photos of Nicole, Dale and Melissa. Meaning he'll target my wife, Nicole. She must stay at Dale and Melissa's farmstead, with over a dozen uniforms guarding her. But I see another photo. That's my sister, Rachel Bradley. Meaning Alonso will put a contract out on Rachel. I'll call her now."

Dave took his cellphone out of the pocket of his leather jacket and dialed Rachel's telephone number. There were five bleeps before she answered.

"Hi there, Rachel Bradley here. Who is it?"

"Rachel, thank God you're okay," Dave said.

"Sure I am. What's the big deal?"

"Rachel, listen very carefully. You must drive to Philadelphia PD and hand yourself into protective custody. You're in danger from Alonso Calvera's mob."

"Are you serious?" Rachel asked.

"Yes, I am," Dave said. "You remember how nearly two years ago, us four FBI agents took down Luis Calvera and his arms dealers who tried to kill us on your farmstead? And you were shot and ended up in hospital?"

"I do remember. What's wrong? You're scaring me."

"Calvera left a son called Alonso. He is running an arms ring and a street gang of hooligans. We've just attacked his hideout here in Timlook, and he has photos on the wall of people he has put out contracts on. People he wants to kill.

"Five attempts have been made to kill me, Tony, Dale and Melissa. He also wants to kill my wife, Nicole. But there was also a photo of you on the wall. Meaning he'll put a contract out on you. Tony, Dale, Melissa and I will travel in a helicopter over to Philadelphia to meet you at the police department. But you must drive there fast, whilst you're still safe."

"Why are you taking a helicopter?" Rachel wanted to know. "Why not Timlook PD's civilian car?"

"A helicopter is faster," Dave explained. "We'll get to you quicker. But you must leave the farmstead immediately and drive to Philadelphia PD."

"Okay, okay," Rachel agreed. "I'll just put some clothes on, skip a shower and breakfast and make my way to Philadelphia PD fast. Goodbye, Dave."

"Goodbye."

Dave ended the call. Then some FBI men in uniforms entered the building.

"You're here at last," Dave remarked.

"We sure are," the FBI inspector replied. "Are you Feds?"

"We are," Dave said. "FBI Agents Dave Bradley and Tony Selma. These dead mobsters were working for arms dealer Alonso Calvera. They paid three corrupt cops including Rulio Diablo to kill us at Melissa's farmstead. The fifth attempt to kill us. Here are photos of us FBI agents, and my sister Rachel. We need a helicopter to pick us up at this farmstead."

"I'll call for a helicopter," the FBI inspector said.

"Our next move?" Tony asked.

"We head for the farmstead," Dave explained. "Whilst I'm driving, you'll text Nicole, telling her we're on our way."

Both FBI agents hurried outside the hideout.

***

At Melissa's farmstead they met up again with Nicole, Dale, Melissa and the uniformed cops.

"You're here at last," Dale said.

"What took you so long?" Melissa asked.

"Make it quick," Nicole said.

"It's a long story," Dave replied.

"We attacked 22 Madrid Street, and got into a shootout with five mobsters," Tony butted in. "We brought them down."

"Then the FBI men arrived," Dave explained, "led by an FBI inspector. Before they arrived, we saw photos of all of us FBI agents, you Nicole and my sister Rachel on Alonso's bedroom wall. Photos he or his men took secretly in public without us or Rachel knowing. He will target Rachel. I made a call to Rachel, telling her to drive to Philadelphia PD and hand herself into protective custody. I asked the FBI inspector to call for a helicopter to pick us up from this farmstead and fly us to Philadelphia PD. And the chopper is coming over now."

"Will the helicopter take five people?" Nicole asked. "You FBI agents and me. Because I see a mass of armed men closing in on us from the north."

"Oh shit!" Dave exclaimed. "They heavily outnumber us!"

In the next few seconds, the helicopter landed and the pilot jumped out, brandishing a rifle.

"You five must get out of here," he suggested. "Including Captain Lamenski."

"Be on your way," the uniformed sergeant ordered. "Us cops will hold off the mobsters."

"Let's go!" Dave cried.

He and Tony led Nicole, Dale and Melissa inside the helicopter, and Dave took the controls.

The mobsters' rifles started blazing at the uniformed cops and the helicopter, but it had already risen above ground and flown away from the farmstead. The cops retaliated with a hail of gunfire, and a savage shootout continued for over ten minutes. Outnumbered and outgunned, the cops and the pilot were riddled full of gunshots and died. But the mobsters also suffered heavy losses, and only eight remained.

***

Inside the helicopter flying toward Philadelphia, Melissa stroked streams of sweat away from her exposed forehead. Dave, Tony and Nicole were also sweating from fear.

"Jesus Christ, that was close!" Melissa shouted.

"You're telling me!" Dale cried.

"Do you think we would've survived that shootout, Dave?" Tony asked.

"No way, Tony," Dave said.

"I reckon none of the uniforms or the pilot survived that," Nicole insisted.

"You reckon right," Tony agreed. "None of them did."

"There's enough fuel here to take us all the way to Philadelphia PD, so we must brace ourselves for a long journey," Dave said. "Even though we're cramped together inside this confined space."

"Rather like five people stuck inside a tank," Dale joked.

"Trust you to be sarcastic," Melissa bantered.

"Don't worry about it." Dave chuckled.

***

Accelerating her car down the side road leading out of the Quaker hamlet, Rachel Bradley speeded toward Philadelphia. But a mobster's car overtook her and rammed its side against her vehicle's side. Rachel cried out with terror. Then a bearded mobster slid open his vehicle's rear side window before aiming his AK-47 assault rifle at Rachel's head. Focusing the lethal weapon, he fired several deadly gunshots, but Rachel ducked and her car swerved.

Her vehicle's front and rear side windows shattered like sheets of ice, and Rachel screamed with petrified terror. Then her car leaped over a ditch and flew into the nearby field, Rachel screaming again. The vehicle crashed upside down in the field, throwing Rachel about between her seatbelt and her seat.

The mobster's vehicle speeded off toward Philadelphia.

"You know what?" the mobster sneered.

"You tell me," the driver said.

"That was a clean kill." The mobster laughed. "Alonso will reward us handsomely."

In the field, Rachel shoved open her vehicle's driver's door and crawled outside onto the grass. She had whiplash and a broken arm, and her face was cut and bruised. Other cars stopped on the curb, and men and women left the vehicles and gathered around Rachel. One man produced his cellphone, dialed 911 and asked the operator for the Philadelphia police and an ambulance.

***

Dave landed the helicopter in Philadelphia PD's car park, and he and Nicole led Tony, Dale and Melissa outside the aircraft. Dave's FBI agents were greeted by a swarm of uniformed men and women led by a smartly dressed man in his fifties with grey hair.

"Hi there," he said. "I'm Captain Luke Kopinski. Are you the FBI agents from Timlook?"

"We are," Nicole asserted. "Sorry to drop in on you in this car park. An unlikely place to land a helicopter. But I'm Captain Nicole Lamenski, head of Timlook PD. My husband here is FBI Agent Dave Bradley. These three FBI agents are Tony Selma, Dale Manuchi and Melissa Morgan. We're strictly here on business."

"We had a long flight." Melissa laughed.

"But we're here at last," Dale said with a chuckle.

"Is my sister, Rachel Bradley, here?" Dave asked.

"Rachel is lying in intensive care at Philadelphia Hospital," Kopinski said.

"In intensive care!" Tony cried.

"What happened?" Dave growled. "Did Alonso's guys get to her before we did?"

"According to drivers who witnessed the shooting," Kopinski explained, "a bearded Cuban fired at her car's side windows, her car careered out of control, jumped a ditch and crashed upside-down in the field. Two other bearded Cubans sat in the back and front seats, but the driver had a moustache. Rachel crawled out of her car and other drivers stopped their cars, ran into the field and helped her. One guy used his cell to call the ambulance and the Philadelphia police."

"Is Rachel okay?" Dave asked.

"She's in a coma," Kopinski told him. "But another driver got the mobsters' car's license plate, our computers did an APB on the vehicle and traced it to one of the mobsters' hideouts."

"The mobsters have more than one hideout then," Nicole commented.

"That doesn't surprise us," Tony remarked. "Where is this hideout?"

"It's number 23 Alberta Avenue," Kopinski informed them. "In northwest Philadelphia on the corner."

"Dale, Melissa and I will head there now," Nicole decided. "Dave and Tony must check on Dave's sister."

"No, Nicole," Dave objected. "You need me and Tony to back up you three."

"Wouldn't you rather check on Rachel at the hospital?" Nicole suggested.

"It makes sense, Dave," Tony told him. "We'll get squad cars to back up Nicole, Dale and Melissa."

"That's not wise," Dale advised Tony. "Squad cars will take away the element of surprise. So will FBI vehicles. It must be just the three of us. You got that?"

"I got it."

"You can give us two civilian cars, and these three cops powerful, high-caliber rifles," Dave said. "They'll drive one vehicle to 23 Alberta Avenue whilst Tony and I take the second vehicle to the hospital."

"Let's go," Nicole ordered the other two.

"And fast," Dave told Dale and Melissa.

"Good luck, Dave and Tony," Kopinski said.

***

At Philadelphia Hospital, Dave and Tony were taken by the nurses to intensive care and approached Rachel's bed. They saw her arm in a sling and the bruises and cuts to her face.

"Oh my God!" Dave exclaimed. He addressed the nurses. "Apart from a broken arm and bruises and cuts to her face, were there any other injuries?"

"Only whiplash," one nurse told him.

"Whiplash!" Tony groaned. "That's deadly serious!"

"Will she be paralyzed?" Dave asked.

"No, Dave," the nurse promised him. "In the operating theatre, top surgeons fixed slight breakages in her spine and neck, but the spinal cord was not damaged. Yet it will be at least a few weeks before we can discharge her from hospital. There's no major damage to her spine or neck, or brain damage."

"She's critical, but stable," another nurse told them. "In case of another attempt on her life by the Cuban mob, we have security guards outside watching over her."

"Thank you for what you've done." Tony praised the doctors and nurses. "The surgeons did a cool job of mending her injuries. And you nurses did well cool."

Dave turned to Rachel, who lay unconscious on the bed.

"We're here now," he told her. "We won't let anything happen to you. And we'll hunt to the ends of the earth to bring to justice the mob who did this to you."

***

Nicole and Melissa were driven by Dale to 23 Alberta Avenue, a posh suburb with a large

Hispanic community, including Mexicans, Puerto Ricans and Cubans.

"You know your way around Philadelphia like the back of your hand," Melissa praised Dale. "You found your way to 23 Alberta Avenue in only ten minutes. Less than that."

"I grew up in Philadelphia and lived here for many years before moving to Timlook," Dale said. "My parents still live in Philadelphia and are now in their late seventies. They live in a care home."

"That explains it." Melissa chuckled. She addressed Nicole. "Drivers who witnessed Rachel's accident said there were four Cubans in the vehicle that rammed her car off the road. The driver was moustached, whilst the other three were bearded, including the man who shot at her side windows. And it looks like only this mobster's vehicle, which had an APB done on the license plate, is in the driveway. No other mobsters' vehicles."

"So only these four mobsters are in the building." Nicole confirmed Melissa's statement. "You and I will take the front."

"And I'll go round the back," Dale said. "Are you ready?"

"We're ready," Melissa replied.

"Step on it," Nicole ordered.

Pushing the civilian car's doors open, they raced outside, shut the doors and sprinted with leopard-like stealth toward 23 Alberta Avenue. Then the front door opened and the four mobsters left the property and approached their vehicle.

Nicole ushered Dale and Melissa back, all three brandishing their rifles. "They haven't seen us. But it's now or never. Let's move."

All three raced toward the mobsters' car and focused their rifles toward the brutes.

"Freeze! Police!"

But the mobsters were fully armed with their AK-47s, and they aimed their dangerous weapons toward Nicole, Melissa and Dale. The detectives wasted no time in retaliating and blasted with their own high-caliber rifles. Nicole blazed two rifle shots toward the mob leader, just as Dale's weapon vomited three gunshots into a second Cuban, and Melissa pumped five rounds into the last two brutes. All four Cubans hurtled onto the driveway, their chests crimson with blood. Dale and Melissa gasped heavily.

"We were up against AK-47 assault rifles, deadly dangerous weaponry in the hands of ruthless mobsters," Dale said.

"It's lucky we had deadly rifles to counter their weapons," Melissa boasted. "Our handguns wouldn't have been nearly as effective."

"Dave will thank us for avenging what these guys did to Rachel," Nicole told the other two. "But Alonso and his guys are still out there. We'll get the FBI to comb this hideout for any new leads to their whereabouts."

"Like their computers?" Dale asked.

"That's the best place to start," Melissa agreed. Her feminine face beamed with a smile.

***

Nicole, Melissa and Dale returned to Philadelphia PD, where they reunited with Captain Kopinski, Dave and Tony.

"Thanks, you three," Dave told them.

"For what?" Nicole asked.

"For saving me the trouble of avenging what these four Cubans did to Rachel," Dave told her.

"It goes with the territory," Dale remarked.

"You're not mad at us, Dave?" Melissa wanted to know.

"Why would he be mad at us?" Nicole objected.

"Cops don't like other cops stealing their thunder," Dale pointed out. "Doing their dirty work for them."

"Quakers like me don't believe in revenge," Dave explained. "Revenge is for the weak. You three saved me the trouble of stopping these sons of bitches from pulling another hit against Rachel. It was justice, not revenge."

"How is your sister?" Nicole asked. "Is she hanging strong?"

"She's critical, but stable," Dave told her.

"Rachel will pull through, because her Quaker faith makes her physically and mentally strong," she assured him.

"You reckon, Nicole?" Melissa asked.

"I reckon," Dale commented.

"The press are here," Dave informed them.

"Excuse me," Nicole said to the journalists. "What are you doing?"

"This is a sensitive case," Captain Kopinski protested. "We don't need the Feds having their faces in the newspapers, showing every arms dealer in Philadelphia these five Timlook detectives are here. Get off our turf."

"Save it, Captain," Tony requested.

"Save it?" Kopinski complained. "The reporters are blowing your covers right out into the open. The Cuban arms dealers will know you're here."

"They already know," Dave told him.

Nicole heard her cellphone bleeping. She took it from her suit jacket and retreated to the captain's office to take the call.

Kopinski turned sharply toward Dave and Tony.

"They already know? How do they know?"

"You want to explain?" Tony asked Dave.

"I will," Dave said. "When Nicole and us FBI agents flew the helicopter away from Melissa's farmstead, a mob of arms dealers massacred the uniforms who covered our escape. These mobsters knew we were flying toward Philadelphia and probably texted Alonso's guys to tell them we were heading for Philly long before we arrived. And the arms dealers who survived the shootout are probably on their way here."

"They are, Dave," Nicole told him. "Eight arms dealers survived the farmstead shootout and may be backing up Alonso's mob here in Philly now."

"Eight more mobsters in Philly!" Dave exclaimed. "How do you know?"

"Your FBI chief Mark Cavitis just mobile called me. More uniforms and FBI people arrived too late to save the uniforms who were massacred, but they also saw the corpses of mobsters who died in the shootout. And they saw eight sets of boot prints leading back toward an enormous truck, which then drove away before the cops arrived, meaning eight mobsters survived the shootout. They would've returned here by now."

"We'll carry out a few sting operations against the arms dealers' hideouts," Dave suggested.

"But first, you must locate their hideouts," Kopinski said.

"What do we have to go on?" Dave asked.

"The computers the FBI took from 23 Alberta Avenue after Dale, Melissa and I had that shootout," Nicole pointed out.

"Information from these computers has been downloaded onto ours," Kopinski said. "You'd better check it out."

***

In the computer room, they spent twenty minutes jotting down information about the mob's addresses throughout Philadelphia.

"You got something?" Kopinski asked.

"Yeah, we have," Tony said.

"We're getting warmer," Nicole said to Dave.

"There are three hideouts in north, south and east Philadelphia," Dave told everybody. "But most of their hideouts are concentrated in and around northwest Philadelphia, including Alberta Avenue. That's where the Hispanic communities go to do business with people within their communities."

"And you know what?" Dale said.

"Alonso's gangs are Cubans," Melissa finished for him.

"So Alberta Avenue is the main business area for the arms dealers and their mobsters," Dave concluded.

"I'll call the Feds, SWAT teams and uniforms to close in on these hideouts," Kopinski declared.

"Jot down the addresses first," Nicole suggested.

"Are you giving me orders?" Kopinski objected.

"It's only advice," Nicole replied. "Sorry, Captain."

"He knows what he's doing," Tony advised her.

"We've already written down the addresses," Dave said.

***

As the FBI agents waited in the main office, uniformed cops brought in newspapers with the agents' photos.

"This ain't good," Dave said when he saw them.

"Too right it ain't good," Tony snapped.

"The whole of Philadelphia knows who we are," Melissa said, "and what we did to those four Cubans." With her dark hair tied back in a ponytail, she wiped beads of sweat from her forehead, then stared seriously at Nicole. Sweat was streaming down her bare forehead and mature face, her grey hair hanging down to her shoulders.

"With our cover blown," Nicole said, "it's best we keep a low profile."

"You mean we hang around here doing nothing?" Dave asked.

"To be blunt, yes. We go out there and we're sitting ducks."

"She's right, Dave, Tony, Melissa," Dale explained. "Just like that shooting that put Rachel in hospital, all it takes is Alonso's guys stopping their vehicles beside our vehicles and pumping several rounds of lead into us from their AK-47s. The four guys Nicole, Melissa and I popped at 23 Alberta Avenue nearly riddled us with their AK-47s."

"We had to act fast," Melissa told Dave.

"We do nothing, the arms dealers and their mob will pump lead into us anyway," Dave complained. "If not today or tomorrow, then the day after. Alonso's guys could walk into this police department now and massacre us with their deadly weapons."

"You think they would be that brazen?" Nicole asked.

"It happened to us at Timlook PD back in 2009," Dave told her. "When we were up against a network of drug cartels called the New England Net. It began when the Mck-Fee brothers in Chicago and Sean Radeski's cartel in Detroit sent their tough guys into Timlook PD to slaughter all of us in a daring hit operation. Radeski and his two co-leaders escaped from the foiled operation; you, Jim and I pursued them to a field, and they escaped in a plane. But I know Alonso's mob is not as brazen as the New England Net were."

"But I know we must take the initiative," Nicole said.

"Then what are we waiting for?" Dave asked.

"We'll approach Captain Kopinski," she said.

***

Nicole and the four FBI agents briefed Captain Luke Kopinski on their plans.

"Look at the arms traffickers and mobsters my men and women have brought into this department," Captain Kopinski said, indicating dozens of arms dealers, mobsters and hooligans from Alonso's street gang being led in handcuffs through the main office and locked up in jail cells. "All these mobsters and youths from street gangs will break under interrogation, and we'll have Alonso Calvera."

"Alonso ain't that stupid," Tony said.

"He'll probably flee from Philadelphia," Melissa informed Kopinski.

"Which means we must hunt him down ourselves," Dale said.

"Before he slips through the net," Dave pointed out. "We'll confiscate the mobsters' cellphones, find Alonso's number, and force the mobsters to arrange a meet with him."

"Then we'll have him," Nicole told Kopinski.

"The hell you will not," Kopinski snapped. "This is not your jurisdiction. This is Philadelphia, not Timlook. You let my teams handle this case, and we'll get back to you. You understand?"

"Hang on, Captain, you're obstructing justice!" Tony cried.

"Alonso has probably found another hideout where we can't find him," Dave said. "We must wait for him to make his next move."

"Dave is right," Nicole asserted. "We must confiscate the mobsters' cellphones and wait for Alonso to call or text them. Then we'll impersonate his mobsters and arrange a meet with him."

"We'll borrow one of Philadelphia PD's civilian cars, and drive to Tandino's Cafe in North Philadelphia, and have a small lunch," Dale suggested.

"We're hungry, and we need to eat," Melissa told Kopinski.

"We'll only eat sandwiches and drinks, not pizzas," Dave said.

"I never said anything about us eating pizzas," Dale objected.

"Good, Detective," Tony growled.

"And whilst we're eating our sandwiches," Dave started.

"We wait for Alonso to make a call," Nicole butted in.

"Okay, you're on it," Kopinski ordered. "You enjoy your sandwiches."

***

At Tandino's Cafe, the five detectives had just finished eating Italian baguettes and drinking glasses of orange juice, pineapple juice and apple juice.

"Did you all enjoy your baguettes?" Dave asked.

"They were horrible," Nicole told him.

"The bread was too hard," Dale said.

"Too stale," Melissa groaned. "But the juices were okay."

"They must've used old bread for the baguettes," Tony told them.

"Okay, okay," Dave said. "But you must try their pizzas. Their pizzas are well cool."

"We've had pizzas here before," Tony told him. "And they are well cool."

"I must try Tandino's pizzas," Nicole said.

"You won't regret it," Tony promised her.

"My cellphone is bleeping," Dave told everybody. "It's Alonso Calvera. How did he get my number? No doubt from Luis Calvera and Ramon Batista. I must answer."

Dave responded to Alonso's call. "Hi Alonso, you son of a bitch! No doubt you got my cellphone number from Luis Calvera? Am I wrong?"

"You're spot on," Alonso snarled. "No thanks to you, most of my mobs and street gangs have been smashed by you motherfucker cops. And I'm smart enough not to contact the mobsters' cellphone numbers. So I'm contacting you, you bastard!"

"Okay, cut the small talk," Dave growled. "Why the call?"

"Listen very carefully," Alonso demanded. "Somebody you care about very much is about to get hurt. Your sister, Rachel. She is in a coma at Philadelphia Hospital, and my men are on their way there to disable her life support machine. If you care about your little sister, then you'd better hurry over to the hospital fast. Good day."

"Hey, wait!" Dave cried. But the line was cut off.

Dave addressed his team. "Alonso's guys are on their way to the hospital to kill Rachel. We must hurry over there now."

"Let's go," Nicole said.

***

At the hospital, they left the civilian car, slammed the doors shut and hurried inside. Dave was frantic and turned to the security guards.

"Have a gang of Cubans come in here?" he asked. "Armed with high-velocity rifles?"

"If they had, we would've shot and killed them," the security guard told him. "But five bearded Cubans came in here and asked to visit Rachel Bradley. Claimed they were FBI men. We directed them to the third floor."

"Melissa and I will stay in reception to intercept any men who try to escape," Nicole ordered. "Dave, Tony and Dale, hurry to the third floor now. The elevator is quicker."

Dave ran toward the elevator with Tony and Dale sprinting behind.

"We have no time to lose!" he shouted.

The elevator opened on the third floor, and Dave, Tony and Dale sped toward the room where Rachel lay unconscious in a bed. Four bearded guys and a moustached man came out of the room and drew their handguns. The FBI agents already had their handguns raised.

"Freeze, FBI!" Dave yelled.

"On the floor!" Dale screamed.

"Go to hell!" the mob leader shouted.

Nurses screamed and dived to the floor as the FBI agents fired before the mobsters.

Dale blasted at two mobsters with three bursts of fire at the same moment Tony blazed two savage blasts at the third guy and Dave's handgun vomited three bullets into the last two, killing the fourth man and wounding the fifth.

"Four mobsters are dead, and the fifth is still alive!" Dale cried.

"Find out from this guy where Alonso's last hideout is," Dave said. "I'll turn on Rachel's life support machine." He hurried into Rachel's room, saw the life support machine turned off, and switched it on again.

"Come on Rachel," he pleaded. "You're doing okay."

Rachel started breathing again.

"You're a fighter, Rachel, so fight for your life."

Then the doctors and nurses entered the room.

"Is she okay?" the head doctor asked.

"I've turned her life support machine back on," Dave told them. "She's breathing. You can take over."

**

Tony and Dale were interrogating the one Cuban still alive.

"Where is Alonso's last hideout?" Dale demanded. "You'd better talk now!"

"Or I'll put a bullet in your leg," Tony growled.

"Grayson Junkyard in west Philadelphia," the mobster said.

"Grayson Junkyard," Tony repeated. He faced Dale. "You know how to find it?"

"I know how to find it," Dale said. "I used to live in Philadelphia. I'll drive."

"I can work out how to find it," Dave objected.

"I'll get us there faster," Dale promised him.

"I'll call Philadelphia PD for backup," Dave said. Pulling out his cellphone, he dialed 911, and Captain Kopinski answered from his office.

"Philadelphia Police Department, Captain Kopinski here. Who's calling?"

"It's FBI Agent Dave Bradley here. We've found out from one of the five mobsters we shot where Alonso Calvera's last hideout is. It's Grayson Junkyard. You know where that is? We need backup there now."

"I'm sending fifteen uniforms over there now," Kopinski said. "They're on their way."

"Thanks, Captain," Dave said. "We're on our way."

He hung up and replaced the mobile inside the pocket of his jeans.

"Let's move," Tony finished off.

***

Inside the civilian car, Tony, Nicole and Melissa sat in the back seats, whilst Dave and Dale were in the front.

"You're sure you know how to find Grayson Junkyard?" Dave asked.

"Trust me, Dave!" Dale insisted. "I know."

"Dale knows Philadelphia like the back of his hand," Melissa chuckled.

"Dave used to live in Philadelphia until he moved to Timlook at the age of twenty-five," Nicole remarked. "It's January 1st, 2022 today, and Dave is approaching fifty-three."

"You look good for it," Tony told him.

"Thanks, young man," Dave said.

Dale raced the civilian car into Grayson Junkyard and crashed into two four-seater vehicles containing the eight mobsters who had survived the shootout at Melissa's farmstead. Dave recognized the Cubans' faces, and all eight mobsters were killed instantly by the devastating impact of the civilian car crashing into their vehicles.

There were three buildings in this junkyard, namely the main office and two warehouses.

"Melissa, come with me into the warehouse on the right," Nicole ordered. "Dale and Tony, you take the left warehouse. Dave will enter the main office, which is probably Alonso's office."

"Alonso's mine," Dave demanded. "I'm doing this for Rachel."

"Good luck, Dave," Tony said.

Pushing open the doors, they hurried outside the car, then sped toward the three buildings, brandishing their handguns. Dave bashed his weight against the main office's door, breaking it open.

"Alonso Calvera!" Dave cried. "It's payback time for what you did to Rachel! Show yourself, Alonso!"

***

In the right warehouse, Nicole and Melissa focused their handguns as they made their way down the aisle. Her dark hair hanging loose down to her shoulders, Melissa used the cuff of her brown leather jacket to swipe a few stray hairs from her eyes so she could see ahead of her.

"You see anybody?" she asked.

"No, I don't," Nicole said. "Wait, I hear footsteps."

"There's three of them," Melissa whispered.

They withdrew behind the shelves flanking the aisle as the Cubans fired at them with their AK-47s. Knowing their handguns were no match for AK-47s, the women waited for the dangerous rifle fire to stop before retaliating.

"Fire now!" Nicole ordered.

Nicole and Melissa emerged from behind the shelves and blasted the mobsters with a ruthless volley of gunfire, shooting them in the back as they ran for the entrance door. Nicole blazed five gunshots which caught one Cuban in his spine and shoulders, breaking through his heart and killing him instantly. Melissa fired five more gunshots toward the other two Cubans, felling one with two shots to his back, then taking down the other brute with three rounds. The bullets sped through the men's hearts and they both died in a matter of seconds.

"Are there any more?" Melissa asked Nicole.

"No more," Nicole replied. "Not bad for two women. Taking out three guys armed with AK-47s."

***

In the left warehouse, Dale and Tony engaged five Cubans.

The crossfire between their handguns and the Cubans' AK-47s was ferocious and brutal, but both FBI agents knew their own weapons could never match AK-47s in firepower. They retreated behind one row of shelves flanking the aisle.

"Their AK-47 assault rifles are too savage," Tony whispered.

"And they're running toward us," Dale said. "Dive to the floor and shoot left, right and center!"

Dale and Tony leaped into the aisle, rolled on the floor and blasted with their weaponry. Tony blazed five shots which sped upward toward two bearded guys. Two rounds penetrated the first man's chest; the other three bullets ploughed into the second guy's solar plexus. With blood gushing down their bodies, both mobsters hurtled to the floor.

Dale fired at the other three Cubans. Two shots struck two men in the chest, and then he pumped four deadly gunshots into the chest and head of a fifth brute. All three men died in seconds, hitting the floor with sickening impact, their chests covered in blood.

***

Inside Alonso's office, Dave searched everywhere before the young arms dealer and his two bodyguards charged out from the washroom and pumped ten shots from their handguns toward Dave, who swiftly dived to the floor. Then Dave aimed his own handgun with brutal accuracy, squeezed the trigger and blazed three shots at the heavies. One shot tore through a man's head whilst the other two rounds penetrated a second killer's chest. Both brutes were thrown to the floor.

Alonso repeatedly fired with intense ferocity and accuracy, pinning Dave behind the desk. Alonso was a professional gunfighter for a young man of only twenty-three, and he fired his own handgun until it ran out of ammunition.

"You have a nerve coming here," he snarled.

"You have a nerve sending gangs of mobsters to kill me in five hit operations," Dave objected. "And putting my sister in hospital."

"You killed my father, Luis Calvera," Alonso growled.

"He had it coming to him," Dave said. "And that makes us even."

As he heard the click of Alonso loading another magazine of bullets, Dave leaped upwards before Alonso could aim. With five terrifying shots from his own weapon, Dave sent a volley of bullets through Alonso's chest and solar plexus, rupturing his sternum, fracturing his spine and puncturing his heart. With dark red blood gushing from his injuries, Alonso crashed against the wall, spun at an angle and hurtled toward the floor. He died three seconds later.

Then Nicole, Tony, Dale and Melissa entered the office, clutching their firearms.

"Did you get Alonso Calvera?" Nicole asked.

"Yeah, I did," Dave gasped. He was fighting to get his breath back.

"You popped two of his heavies too," Tony observed.

"You alone against three men," Melissa bantered.

"Talk about balancing being a Quaker with being a cop." Dale laughed.

"They were professionals, and they almost killed me," Dave said, his voice fearful. "They took me by surprise, and I only ducked in the nick of time. Alonso's desk shielded me. Then I popped the two heavies, and before Alonso loaded his gun, I fired five lucky shots into him. For a kid of twenty-three, Alonso Calvera was the most dangerous gunman in the entire mob."

"He had that in common with his father, Luis Calvera," Tony explained. "Alonso's brutality, his arms trafficking gangs and street gangs, and his proficiency with weapons made him by far the most dangerous arms dealer on the East Coast. With a reputation which rivaled his father's."

"He was loading his handgun," Dave said, "and I got lucky."

Then fifteen uniformed cops swarmed into the junkyard.

"You're rather late!" Tony shouted.

"We got held up in traffic," the sergeant explained.

"We saved you a tough job," Dave remarked.

***

A few weeks later, Rachel was discharged from Philadelphia Hospital and was back at the Quaker farmstead outside Lancaster County. In her farmhouse, she sat at her dining room table with Dave and Nicole on one side and Tony, Dale and Melissa on the other.

"Okay, everybody," Dave announced. "Let's praise my sister Rachel for a remarkable recovery."

"Thank you, Dave," Rachel said. "Shall I pour the wine?"

"No, you will not," Tony objected. "Your arm is still mending itself."

"Let me pour the wine," Dale said.

"You're such a gentleman, Dale, honey," Melissa praised him.

"You're lucky to have a husband like Dale," Nicole told her.

"And you're lucky to have a husband like Dave." Tony complimented the bearded Quaker.

"Dale is pouring the wine." Rachel chuckled.

"Thanks, Dale," Dave said.

"Serving drinks is an art," Nicole pointed out.

"And there's somebody at the door," Rachel said.

"I'll get it." Dave got up, walked to the front door and opened it.

Standing outside was Captain Kopinski and four uniformed cops.

"Hi there, everybody," all five greeted them.

Then Kopinski took over, with his praise of how Nicole and the FBI agents had smashed

Alonso Calvera's arms trafficking ring. "You nailed Alonso Calvera and his mobsters. You guys and ladies deserve a special promotion from your people at the top back in Timlook."

"Thank you, Kopinski," Dave responded. "But we don't want a promotion. Our place is on the street bringing criminals to justice. But thanks again. Do you want some wine?"

What Did You Think of *No Greater Evil* and *No Greater Wickedness?*

A big thank you for purchasing this book. It means a lot that you chose this book specifically from such a wide range on offer. I do hope you enjoyed it.

Book reviews are incredibly important for an author. All feedback helps them improve their writing for future projects and for developing this edition. If you are able to spare a few minutes to post a review on Amazon, that would be much appreciated.

Publisher Information

Rowanvale Books provides publishing services to independent authors, writers and poets all over the globe. We deliver a personal, honest and efficient service that allows authors to see their work published, while remaining in control of the process and retaining their creativity. By making publishing services available to authors in a cost-effective and ethical way, we at Rowanvale Books hope to ensure that the local, national and international community benefits from a steady stream of good quality literature.

For more information about us, our authors or our publications, please get in touch.

www.rowanvalebooks.com
info@rowanvalebooks.com

www.ingramcontent.com/pod-product-compliance
Lightning Source LLC
Chambersburg PA
CBHW040016250626
47171CB00005B/25